A CUPID'S BOW, TEXAS REUNION

— ✖ —

TANYA MICHAELS

HARLEQUIN® HOME ON THE RANCH

Recycling programs
for this product may
not exist in your area.

ISBN-13: 978-1-335-83487-4
ISBN-13: 978-1-335-04186-9 (Direct to Consumer edition)

Home on the Ranch: A Cupid's Bow, Texas Reunion

Printed in U.S.A.

www.Harlequin.com

"Layla?" He frowned in concern. Then he paled. "Oh, God."

The dawning suspicion in his expression made her feel as powerless and nauseated as if she were watching a car accident happen. No no no no. Her lungs constricted. For a split second, she thought she might actually pass out.

"How old is she, exactly? How old is your daughter?"

She wished she could pass out. The oblivion of unconsciousness would be a blessing right now. The sweetness of strawberries in the back of her throat suddenly tasted like every nightmare she'd ever had.

Jace shook his head in denial even as his eyes narrowed in accusation. "She's not...mine, is she? I sound like a crazy person. Of course she's not! You would have told me."

"I'm sorry." Tears began to spill over her cheeks. "Jace, I am s-so, so sorry." Then she was out of the booth, nearly crashing into a waitress.

Dear Reader,

If this is your first trip to Cupid's Bow, Texas, welcome! I'm so glad you made it—and don't worry, each of the stories in my fictional small town is a stand-alone read that can be enjoyed on its own. (But I hope you'll be inspired to check out some of the other Cupid's Bow books!)

For those of you who have been to Cupid's Bow before, thank you, thank you, thank you for taking this journey with me. I have loved your online reviews, your comments on Twitter and your Facebook questions about when the next Cupid's Bow book would be released.

This is my final book in the series, so I was delighted to have a plot that allowed me to revisit so many familiar characters. The very first Cupid's Bow book introduced Sheriff Cole Trent, and we met his younger brother, perpetual bachelor Jace. Now Jace Trent is a little older, a little wiser and ready to follow his heart. However, the object of his affection—a longtime friend who's only recently returned to Cupid's Bow—seems intent on avoiding him. Single mom Layla Dempsey has always adored Jace, but she has a secret to keep. If he finds out the truth about her daughter, will Jace ever forgive her?

I'd love to know what you think of this last Cupid's Bow story! Please join me on Facebook or Twitter to chat about this book and to stay updated on my future releases.

Best wishes,

Tanya

Tanya Michaels, a bestselling author and eight-time RITA® Award finalist, has written more than forty books full of love and laughter. Tanya is a popular event speaker, an unrepentant Netflix addict and a mother of two. She lives outside Atlanta with two teenagers who inherited her quirky sense of humor and a spoiled bichon frise who has no idea that she's a dog.

Books by Tanya Michaels

Harlequin Western Romance

Cupid's Bow, Texas

Falling for the Sheriff
Falling for the Rancher
The Christmas Triplets
The Cowboy Upstairs
The Cowboy's Texas Twins

Harlequin American Romance

Hill Country Heroes

Claimed by a Cowboy
Tamed by a Texan
Rescued by a Ranger

The Colorado Cades

Her Secret, His Baby
Second Chance Christmas
Her Cowboy Hero

Visit the Author Profile page
at Harlequin.com for more titles.

The heart of my Cupid's Bow series is community, and I couldn't have written this book without the community of women who helped me through the hardest year of my life. Beth, Jane, Lara, Maggie, Melissa, Missy, Sally, Susan and Trish—I love you guys! Special thanks also to Johanna and Pam. And to Wade Wilson, for always making me laugh.

Chapter 1

"Mama, don't leave me!" The little girl's wail was dramatic enough that diners at nearby tables whipped their heads around to investigate.

Ignoring glances from former neighbors and acquaintances, Layla Dempsey sat back down. "We talked about this, Addie. I just need an hour or two to visit Uncle Chris in the hospital—which is a very boring place. Instead of waiting there, you get to watch a movie and color pictures with Gena."

Addie's blue eyes widened, and her lower lip trembled. "But I don't know Gena. She's a *stranger*."

Layla shot an apologetic look toward her cousin, praying that Addie wasn't about to alienate their biggest ally in town by shrieking *Stranger danger!* at top volume. *Please, God, no epic meltdowns today.* Though she loved her six-year-old daughter unconditionally, Layla's nerves were already shot from coming home to Cupid's Bow. *And your daughter is picking up on all that tension.* If Addie was on edge, Layla was partially to blame.

Deep breaths. Layla reached inside her giant purse—more backpack than pocketbook—and pulled out the "twinkle jar." It was a plastic bottle she and Addie had filled with water, liquid soap, multicolored glitter and a few sparkly beads. Layla had superglued the lid, and now the bottle functioned almost like a lava lamp. Addie could turn it this way and that, watching the beads slowly travel through the dense liquid as the glitter shifted in soothing, ever-changing formations. The bottle often helped distract Addie from her anxiety.

In a reassuring tone, Layla said, "I know you don't like unfamiliar situations, but this restaurant today was new, right? You'd never been here before and you didn't know if you would like it." She nodded toward the girl's empty plate. "Wasn't the food good?"

Addie almost smiled, the corner of her mouth still smeared with barbecue sauce. "Yummy."

"And Cousin Gena's house is unfamiliar, but you're going to like her, too." It might have been better if Layla had driven to the house to get her daughter settled in, but Gena lived clear on the other side of town and Layla had spent enough time behind the wheel today. They'd compromised by meeting for lunch close to the hospital. "She's not only family, she was my best friend growing up."

Gena nodded. "I have scrapbooks with lots of pictures of your mom. Want to see what she looked like when she was your age?"

After a moment's thought, Addie nodded.

"And maybe you can scope out my house," Gena

coaxed, "to help me decide the best place to go in case of a bad storm?"

"You mean like a tornado?" Now Addie was hooked. Ever since a tornado drill her first week of kindergarten, she'd been morbidly fascinated. For the past few months, she'd carried two children's books about twisters everywhere she went and watched the opening scenes from *The Wizard of Oz* on a near-daily basis—but she lost interest in the movie the minute Dorothy touched down in Munchkinland. On the occasional afternoons when Layla had to bring her daughter to the photography studio, Addie kept herself busy by looking up tornado facts on kid-friendly educational sites. At first, Layla had tried to discourage the fixation, but since memorizing and reciting statistics seemed to calm her daughter...

"Do you have a basement?" Addie asked.

Gena shook her head. "Afraid not."

"What about a room with no windows? Like a big closet. But not upstairs. Down is safer." As she relayed these facts, her voice grew more confident, the earlier panic in her expression gone.

"There aren't any stairs at my house," Gena said, "so we're good on that count. But I'd love your opinion on whether the walk-in pantry or laundry room would be better."

"You need my help." Addie reached for her jacket, clearly eager to get started.

The relief that flooded Layla was so strong she felt almost giddy until she remembered where she was headed and why. "You be good, Addie Rose." The girl's car seat and backpack were already waiting in Gena's Mustang. "I'll see you by four o'clock." Probably sooner, but better to be early than to have Addie fretting because her mother was late.

"We'll be fine," Gena said. "My neighbor has a daughter her age, and I've always survived babysitting."

"I owe you big-time."

Her cousin winked at her. "Add it to the tab."

How would I ever begin to pay that? Gena had done her countless favors over the years. As kids, they'd been as close as sisters—and often mistaken for siblings. They had similar builds and the same naturally curly brown hair. Layla studied the image of the three of them reflected in the exit door. Addie, standing between them, was cut from the same genetic cloth, her mother in miniature form, except that Addie Rose didn't have the hazel eyes that ran in the family. She'd inherited her dad's blue eyes.

Layla's palms went clammy, her stomach tightening. She hurried outside, wanting the cool autumn air against her skin. The guilty secret she'd kept from everyone, even Gena, was a fever that always burned worse here in Cupid's Bow. At seventeen, when she'd lied about the identity of Addie's father, she'd been in a panic, not wanting to ruin his life just as he'd left for college, his future wide open. She hadn't stopped to consider the long-term viability of her deception. Instead, she'd seized her parents' bitter divorce as an excuse to flee Cupid's Bow, choosing to live with her dad and staying out of town for as long as possible.

Given a chance to do it all again, would she make different decisions?

As a teenager, she'd loved Jace Trent with all her heart—their families forcing them to marry for the baby's sake might have held some fantasy allure. But, one hot summer night notwithstanding, Jace hadn't felt the same way about her. A forced marriage would have caused him to resent the hell out of her, and she'd seen from her own parents how much two spouses could come to hate each other. Besides, her big brother Chris would have beaten his best friend to a pulp if he'd ever learned who got her pregnant. Seducing Jace had been her idea; she hadn't wanted to be the reason a lifelong friendship ended.

I could always tell Chris the truth while I'm here. Based on the medical updates from Layla's sister-in-law, it would be months before Chris was in any shape to land a punch. Her rodeo champion brother had fallen off a bull, his worst injuries sustained when the bull stepped on him. She was anxious to see with her own eyes that he was recovering.

Layla made it to the hospital in a matter of minutes, but dread slowed her movements as she walked toward the entrance. Would she run into her mother here? Layla would prefer to have that reunion privately, to avoid another scene like the one at Chris and Suzanne's wedding reception three years ago.

Had Mom finally forgiven her daughter's *disloyal abandonment* or how Layla had *shamed her family* by getting knocked up in high school? Hoping for the best, Layla walked through the automatic doors.

She wrinkled her nose at the vaguely chemical smell and the overly bright decorating touches—orange padded benches and neon murals on the walls. Following Suzanne's directions, she took an elevator to the third floor and turned down a corridor. Even before she reached the enclosed waiting room, Layla glimpsed familiar faces through the floor-to-ceiling glass. Former rodeo champion Jarrett Ross paced the small room, looking uncharacteristically pale beneath his year-round tan; he and Chris were close friends despite the many times they'd competed against one another. The two handsome black men seated on opposite benches were the Washington brothers, Hugh and Quincy. She'd heard Hugh had walked away from rodeo life after getting married, but Quincy held current state records in bronc riding.

All three men turned toward her when she entered the room, and Layla quickly found herself at the center of a group hug. Tears stung her eyes. Despite the life she'd worked hard to build for herself and her daughter in Austin, there were so many people she missed here in Cupid's Bow.

Rising up on her tiptoes, she kissed each Washington brother on the cheek. "How's your mom?" Rita Washington was Layla's all-time favorite high school teacher and had continued to email her even after Layla moved away and gossip spread about her disgraceful pregnancy.

Quincy rolled his eyes. "On my case to find a nice girl and settle down."

Hugh shook his head. "Getting married doesn't stop the lectures. She's on *my* case to give her grandbabies." He winked at Layla. "Doesn't help that your brother and Suzanne have adorable twin babies. It's giving Mama ideas."

Poor Suzanne, trying to take care of four-month-old daughters while worried about her husband in the hospital. Still, she'd tried her best to sound positive when she updated Layla on the phone. "He's young and strong and surgery went well. Cupid's Bow has a new physical therapist who's incredible—she's worked with other rodeo cowboys. Not to mention, she married one."

Layla poked Jarrett in the side. "I hear you're a newly-wed. Congratulations!"

His lips quirked in a half smile, but the fleeting grin didn't ease the tension in his face. He shifted his weight, looking as uncomfortable and fidgety as Addie Rose when she'd been in the car for longer than ten minutes.

"Are you okay?" Layla asked, unnerved by his expression. "Has there been news on Chris, or—"

"Your brother's fine," Jarrett hastily assured her. "I mean, not *fine*, obviously, a bull stepped on him and he has four broken bones and spinal—"

"Dude," Quincy said under his breath.

Jarrett winced. "Sorry, Layla. I'm rattled. I really hate hospitals. Maybe I should excuse myself, go get a cup of coffee or something."

"Decaf," Hugh suggested. "You're jittery enough already."

"Want to come with me?" Jarrett asked her. "Suzanne just went back to talk to the doctors, so it'll probably be another five or ten minutes before any of us are allowed into the room."

"Is my mom here, too?"

Hugh shook his head. "She was here yesterday but she sounds like she's coming down with a cold. Suzanne told her she should stay home and rest today. Claire's barely slept since last weekend."

"I bet Suzanne hasn't, either," Layla said, swamped with sympathy for her sister-in-law.

"That's why we come by every day," Jarrett said, "to let her run home and take a nap without Chris being left alone. And Hugh and his wife have been babysitting the twins as much as possible."

"We all wish we could do more," Quincy added.

He was known for being the mischievous Washington brother, but at the moment, he radiated somber sincerity.

"My brother's lucky to have such good friends." Trying to inject a little levity, Layla added, "And such good-*looking* friends. Y'all know you're abnormally hot, right?"

Quincy smirked. "We know…but feel free to expand on the topic." The other two men laughed.

Relieved to have lightened the mood, she turned back to Jarrett. "Guess I could use some coffee, too. Got up pretty early. Hugh, Quincy, should we bring anything back for you?" She asked the question over her shoulder, already moving toward the door—until she collided with a well-muscled chest.

"Hey, beautiful."

The blood went ice-cold in her veins as she registered Jace Trent's voice. She forced herself to turn, meeting a pair of blue eyes that were the exact shade of her daughter's. Those eyes crinkled as Jace smiled, apparently oblivious to her sudden urge to throw up on his boots.

She tried to make her lips form an answering smile, but instead heard herself blurt, "What the hell are you doing here?"

Chapter 2

Startled by Layla's unwelcoming tone, Jace rocked back on his heels. "I'm visiting your brother?" He didn't usually sound uncertain of his own statements, but everything about the brunette standing in front of him left him off-balance. The last time he'd seen her had been at Chris and Suzanne's wedding. She'd been withdrawn, which Jace had attributed to an unflattering bridesmaid's dress and arguing with her mom, but now Layla was downright hostile.

She was also gorgeous.

She'd been a pretty teenager, but she'd been skinny and often at war with her curly hair, trying unsuccessfully to tame it into conformity. Now it spilled over her shoulders in spirals he wanted to tug between his fingers. In a pair of jeans and a black knit top that clung to womanly curves, she—

"I meant, what are you doing here in Cupid's Bow?" Layla stepped backward, her voice softer. She didn't look thrilled to see him, but at least she was no longer glaring. "Last I heard, you were following some job lead to a ranch in Colorado."

Had he imagined that she was angry at his presence? Maybe she was just tense because of her brother's injuries, and Jace had been wrong to take it personally. "The Colorado thing didn't pan out."

Behind them, Quincy snorted. "You know how Jace is—always bouncing between jobs and opportunities."

"And women," Jarrett added.

Being friends with these guys was like being kicked by a mule. "Ha ha," Jace drawled. "Y'all are hilarious."

Hugh exchanged a look with his brother. "Who was joking?"

"I manage the tack-and-supply store now," Jace told Layla. "I'm half owner and pretty serious about making my investment back."

"And women?" she asked, not quite meeting his gaze. "Is there one you're serious ab— Never mind. None of my business."

"He just broke up with someone last month," Quincy said.

"I…" Jace wasn't sure how much he wanted to explain about that. Or why he cared so much what Layla's opinion would be. He hadn't seen her in three years. And, if she didn't make peace with her mother, it could easily be another three years before anyone in Cupid's Bow saw her again. Still, he and Layla had been close once upon a time. He had a nostalgic urge to confide in her, to tell her what had happened with his last relationship.

"You're here!" Emerging from the doorway at the

other side of the waiting room, Suzanne Dempsey broke into a jog, nearly tackling Layla in her excitement. "Come on back—Chris will be *so* happy to see you." She cast a glance at the men standing around. "Y'all don't mind waiting a little longer, do you? They discourage everyone from piling in at once."

"Hey, we're here for you," Jarrett said. "Want us to wait, we will. Want us to go out and grab you some non-hospital food for lunch, we're on it."

Gratitude lit Suzanne's face. "These guys have been the best," she told Layla. "I don't know what I would have done without them. You must have been the luckiest girl in all of Cupid's Bow to grow up with so many honorary big brothers."

Layla's gaze collided with Jace's and her cheeks went bright red before she quickly looked away.

The old guilt twisted in his chest. On that long-ago steamy July night, his actions toward her sure as hell hadn't been brotherly. In the days afterward, he'd hated himself a little, feeling as if he'd betrayed his friendship to her as well as his friendship with Chris. If he and Chris had gone to the same college, Jace probably would have ended up admitting his sins in an ill-advised, beer-fueled confession. By the time Jace moved back to Cupid's Bow, he hadn't seen Layla in such a long time he could almost pretend that night had never happened. *Almost.*

But now, with her standing only a few feet away, suppressed recollections flooded his senses. The smell of honeysuckle and the distant rumble of an approaching storm, the way Layla's touches had been soft and tentative at first, at odds with the resolve in her voice.

Then she'd grown bold, eager for him, and he'd lost his damned mind.

What is wrong with you? Past mistakes aside, he had no business lusting after his best friend's sister—especially not when said best friend was laid up in a hospital bed down the hall. Perhaps it would be best to avoid being alone with Layla while she was here in town.

But could he avoid his own memories of the night they'd shared?

Layla followed her sister-in-law out of the waiting room, trying to keep her pace normal. She didn't want to look as if she was fleeing…even though one smile from Jace had been enough to trigger her fight-or-flight response. Her heartbeat thundered so loudly in her ears that she only heard every third word Suzanne said.

As Suzanne explained Chris's current medical situation, they passed a nurse's station where a blonde in scrubs was boxing up smiling plush jack-o-lanterns and a man on a ladder was removing cute ghost posters from the wall. November was a time for people to be thankful, to count their blessings; Layla's outlook was bittersweet. She knew Chris's injuries could have been worse—thank God they weren't—but she hated that he and Suzanne were going through this mere months after Suzanne's difficult pregnancy and the twins' birth. Layla couldn't imagine what the medical bills would be like.

Suzanne pointed to a door on the left. "Here we are. He had a roommate, but Patrick checked out yesterday."

She was sure her brother was anxious to do the same. "When will Chris get to go home?"

"The doctors are hoping for the day after tomorrow, but it's too soon to tell."

From the slow way Suzanne said the words and the confused look on her face, Layla realized her sister-in-law must have already told her that.

"Sorry. I was preoccupied. Worrying."

"I get it, trust me. The first time the doctors talked to me after surgery, it was just meaningless noise. If your mom hadn't been there to ask the right questions and repeat the details for me later… Have you talked to her since you got to Cupid's Bow?"

Was Layla imagining the note of censure in Suzanne's tone? "I texted her that Addie and I made it safely to town. I wanted to check on Chris as soon as possible. I'll call Mom tonight." *And won't that be fun?* Trying to squelch her dread, Layla reached past her sister-in-law to open the door. "Hope you're decent, bro! Womenfolk are entering the room."

Chris snorted. "Have you ever tried to be 'decent' in a hospital gown? It's not possible."

The fact that he sounded like his usual self was the only thing that kept her from crying when she got her first look at him. Chris had always been her strong big brother. Now he was covered in bruises with a cast on his right leg, bandaging around his skull and two of his fingers taped together. The accident had only been a few days ago, but he'd already lost weight. His face looked too thin beneath the scruffy beginnings of a beard.

"Hey," he said impatiently. "I'm not dying. Quit looking at me like there should be a priest giving last rites."

Layla forced a smile. "Well, you can understand my confusion. You always told me you were invincible, unbreakable, a supergenius and pretty much the definition of perfection."

"Guess I forgot to tell the bull. Now come give your brother a hug—gently."

Blinking hard, she did as ordered. She hadn't felt so nervous about accidentally hurting someone since she'd brought a newborn Addie home from the hospital.

With his good hand, Chris patted her upper arm. "You see what I'm willing to go through just to get my only sibling to visit me?"

Ouch. That statement hit home. Since Suzanne's parents lived about twenty minutes from Layla, she'd benefitted from the times Chris visited his in-laws. But she almost never set foot in Cupid's Bow.

It was on the tip of her tongue to promise she'd do better in the future, but, frankly, now that she knew Jace Trent lived here again, she'd be a nervous wreck any time she was within the city limits. She'd almost hyperventilated when he spoke to her at Chris's wedding reception, and that had been a mere three-minute encounter. She'd managed to mostly avoid him, a task made easier by his flirting with a hot bridesmaid.

How long would she be able to avoid him while she was in town? He knew that she had a daughter, but what if he actually met Addie? He might ask Addie's age. The math was fairly self-explanatory, unless he believed the lie she'd told her family.

"Layla? Earth to my kid sister?"

That got her attention. She rolled her eyes at Chris. "You're only a year and a half older. And neither of us are kids anymore."

"Where'd your mind wander?" he asked. "I don't think you heard a thing we said."

Suzanne frowned. "You zoned out earlier, too."

"I'm just tired. I'll be better tomorrow after a good

night's rest." Ha! As if she'd be able to sleep a wink to-night. "Is there anything I can bring you when I come back? Extra pillow? Candy bars? Dirty magazines like the ones you used to hide from Mom?"

He looked sheepishly at his wife. "I was young and stupid then. You know I have the utmost respect for women." To Layla, he said, "There is one thing I could use, since you're offering. Be a dear and rob Cupid's Bow First National Bank for me. I need a rental wheel-chair and your nieces need college funds."

She pretended to think it over. "Our cousin *is* a teller there. I suppose Gena can get me the blueprints and guard schedule. But I'm only doing the robbery if I get to drop suspended from the ceiling *Mission-Impossible-*style," Layla said. "It's my chance to finally be cool."

"Hey, you're related to *me*," he said. "It doesn't get any cooler than that."

"Oh yeah?" Layla smirked but lost track of what she'd been about to say when she noticed Suzanne's pinched expression.

Chris followed her gaze. "Honey, what is it? Because I made the joke about money?" He reached for his wife's hand. "I was kidding—you know me. We're going to be okay—I promise."

"Sure." Her breath hitched, and she rubbed her knuck-les under her eyes. "I—I know that."

"Come here. You and I are going to get through this."

Suzanne leaned down to hug him, burying her face in the crook of his neck, and he murmured low re-assurances Layla couldn't hear. She swallowed past the lump in her throat, moved by their obvious love for each other. They were a team, an unshakable unit. Layla was doing the best she could as a single parent, but there were nights she tossed and turned, wishing—

No. This was not the time or place for self-pity. She was here to help Chris and Suzanne… If only she could figure out a tangible way to do that. She empathized with what Quincy had said. *We all wish we could do more.* Her brother had very loyal friends.

Loyal, attractive cowboy friends.

Layla suddenly smiled. *I might just have an idea.*

Chapter 3

"How much would I pay for a shirtless cowboy?" Gena repeated the question with some confusion as she stirred the spaghetti sauce.

"Twelve cowboys!" Layla rubbed her hands together, enthusiasm a buzz in her system. "Or three of them, four times? I haven't really done the math yet. Group shots? Six, twice each?"

Gena darted a glance to where Addie was watching the opening credits of *The Wizard of Oz* in the next room, then lowered her voice. "Um…did you help yourself to some unauthorized meds at the hospital? You're not making much sense."

Layla crossed the kitchen to pour herself a glass of water, trying to get her thoughts in order. "The toughest thing about seeing Chris in the hospital was feeling helpless. There's so little I can do for them. And I know other people feel the same way. Jarrett Ross was in the waiting room with the Washington brothers. Everyone wants to help, but it's not like any of us are swimming in millions. Then I remembered this charity calendar I did last year, photographing hunky local firefighters."

Gena sighed wistfully. "Your job is so much better than mine."

"They sold the calendars to raise money for the fire department. Why couldn't we do something like that? I'll do all the photography, and if we can get the printing donated, people will have plenty of time to buy calendars before the New Year."

"Your brother does have very attractive friends. Jarrett and Quincy and Jace and—"

"Jace." Layla's stomach dropped. She'd been so excited about a possible way to help her brother's family that she'd overlooked the obvious. Once she started asking for volunteers, Jace Trent would want to be involved; he'd been Chris's best friend since grade school. The idea of working with him…seeing him without his shirt…touching him as she helped position him for the best light and framing… "I, uh, heard he's busy as the co-owner of a store. Maybe he won't have time?"

"Are you kidding? For Chris, he'll make the time. Besides, he might even agree to carry the calendars in the store, which would be a huge help. Cowboy calendars go right along with all the rodeo and equestrian gear he sells."

It would be helpful, having them stocked in an actual store. She hadn't thought that far ahead yet, but local vendors seemed more effective than trying to sell calendars out of the trunk of her car. *You can do this—for Chris. You're a grown woman, and that night with Jace was a lifetime ago.* It wasn't as if she'd be bringing Addie to the photo shoots. "Well, it's all a moot point until I figure out printing costs. If we can't turn a significant profit, there's no sense going through the trouble. And I want to give Hugh and Jarrett time to talk to their wives, make sure everyone is all right with the idea."

"Another reason why Jace is an ideal candidate. I hear he just broke up with his latest girlfriend. Good thing for Mrs. Trent that her other two sons are happily married, providing her grandkids to spare. That youngest of hers is never going to settle down."

A half-dozen questions about Jace's personal life tumbled through Layla's mind, but she refused to voice any of them. She had zero claim on Jace Trent. Her birthday wish the summer she'd turned seventeen was one night to remember him by. When she'd worked up the courage to make it happen weeks later, she'd told him she wanted a first time with someone she cared about, without strings. Without complications.

In the living room, Addie cheered for Toto, and Layla's heart twisted. Her night with Jace hadn't been uncomplicated, but she would never be sorry. Blindly in love with the boy who'd been the bright spot of her life during her parents' awful divorce, she'd wanted Jace to give her a few hours of pleasure. Instead, he'd unknowingly given her the gift of a lifetime.

A gift he's missing out on. She chewed the inside of her lip. Would telling him now do more harm than good? How would she even go about it? *Would you like to see a picture of my daughter? Oh, by the way, she has your eyes.*

"Are you okay?" Gena asked. "You went from talking so fast I couldn't follow what you were saying to eerily quiet."

"Just mulling over this calendar idea."

"Want to chop veggies for salad while you mull?"

"Sure."

Layla was retrieving cucumbers and carrots from the fridge when the phone rang.

Behind her, Gena answered with a hello and a pause. "Um, yeah. She's right here. Layla, it's for you."

Mom. Well, this had been inevitable. She might as well get it over with. Holding out her hand, she mouthed to Gena, "My mother?"

"Much better." Gena grinned. "Jace Trent."

Layla's stomach churned like an entire line of tornados had just blown through her. She hoped Gena hadn't gone to much trouble making the spaghetti; there was no way Layla would be able to eat. "H-hello?"

"Hi, beautiful." There was no flirtation in the word, just habit. Jace had called her that even when she'd been a frizzy-haired thirteen-year-old with braces. No wonder she'd gone all starry-eyed over him, daring to hope he might someday return her feelings.

"Mama!" From the living room, Addie's exasperated tone let her know that the "good part" of the movie had passed.

Layla went cold in the irrational fear that Jace might somehow guess his paternity just by hearing his daughter's voice in the distance. "Um, Jace, hold on." She set the phone on the counter, glad for the moment's reprieve to compose herself.

Addie was glowering at the remote to the DVD player. Gena's was a bit more high-tech than the one they had at home. "I don't know these buttons. Can you restart it?"

"S-sure, baby."

"Why do you sound like that?"

Layla wished she could ignore the question, but she knew from experience how persistent her daughter was. "Like what?"

"I don't know. Funny. Like when I played tag with Meredith and ran too fast and it made my tummy hurt."

"You are exactly right. I do have a stomachache."

"Are you gonna hafta drink the pink stuff? Yuck."

"I'm not sure yet. But I haven't ruled it out."

Addie patted her hand sympathetically. "I love you, Mommy."

"Love you, too." And unless she wanted her daughter's already fragile world turned upside down, she would get back on that phone with Jace Trent and act like nothing was wrong.

Layla wasn't a deceptive person by nature—but for her daughter's sake, she would stick by the lies she'd told. Even Jace's closest friends described him as someone who quickly grew bored with a girlfriend or a career after a few weeks. Parenting was a lifelong commitment, one she'd assured him wasn't a risk. Part of her naive seduction plan had included birth control pills, but she'd overlooked the necessity of taking them for seven days before trusting their effectiveness.

She tried to sound casual when she greeted Jace again. "Sorry about that. Duty called."

"No problem. I can be patient."

Too bad. It would have been simpler if he'd hung up and gone away. "What can I do for you?"

"Other way around. I wanted to do something for you. Chris said you probably won't see your mom until tomorrow. I thought you might not want to face her alone. My mother loves any reason to throw a dinner. I could suggest she invite—"

"Jace, that's sweet." She was moved by his un-expected thoughtfulness, but it shouldn't come as such a surprise. He'd always been kinder than necessary to Chris's tagalong little sister. "But I'm afraid we'd just end up causing a scene. Your family doesn't need that." She sure as hell couldn't bring Addie to dinner with the people most likely to spot any childhood resemblance to a young Jace.

"My family is tough. It takes a lot to rattle the Trents."

That was true. One of his older brothers was the sher-iff, and the other was a fireman. They were brave men, beloved in the community, but it had always been Jace with his teasing smile and bright blue eyes who'd been her favorite.

"I don't want to be pushy," he said, "but I'm not used to taking no for an answer. We have that in common."

She swallowed hard. Was he talking about her stub-born nature in general or the night she'd overcome his perfunctory protests and convinced him to take her vir-ginity? "It's a bad idea."

He sighed. "Call me if you change your mind?"

"Sure." Not a chance.

"Actually, call me for any reason. You may not look back on your departure from Cupid's Bow fondly, but there are still people here who care about you."

She knew the soft words were meant to be reassuring, but they filled her with self-loathing. *Don't be nice to me. You don't know what I've done.*

And, unfortunately, she had to keep it that way.

I must be losing my touch. Scowling, Jace tossed his cell phone onto the couch cushion next to him. There'd been a time, not so long ago, when he'd been known for his ability to charm women of all ages. His brothers often asked him to intercede when they had bad news to give their mother. Jace's business partner, Grayson Cox, joked that he'd hired Jace solely because the ladies in town would line up to buy stuff from him.

The fabled Jace Trent charm, however, hadn't kept his girlfriend from dumping him last month. And now Layla Dempsey seemed one-hundred-percent immune to him. Clearly, she wasn't struggling with the same intimate memories he was. That realization stung.

Scowling, he stood. It wasn't as if he'd thought Layla was pining after him all these years later. He didn't even want that. He just wanted... Well, he wasn't entirely sure.

Still, he'd been irrationally disappointed by her rejection tonight. Inviting her to dinner with his family had seemed like a safe way for them to catch up without violating his resolve not to be alone with her. Could she have sounded less interested in rekindling their friendship?

You are really on a roll lately. He went into the kitchen, wondering if he had anything in the fridge resembling dinner. He hadn't had his usual appetite in the weeks since Kelli had ended their relationship. It wasn't so much that he was heartbroken as he was dissatisfied with his life.

Until Kelli's pregnancy scare, he hadn't even realized that he wanted more. When the stick had come up with a negative sign, she'd been joyfully relieved but he'd felt hollow. In the few minutes while they'd been waiting for the results, he'd thought about his nieces and nephew. He'd allowed himself to imagine a life like the lives his happily married brothers led—settled with a woman who adored him, raising bright, energetic kids. For the first time, Uncle Jace felt ready to be a father. But when he'd told Kelli that, she'd been horrified. She'd said they were in very different places and dumped him flat.

It's been a few weeks. You should throw your hat back into the dating ring. But he had even less enthusiasm for that idea than he did for grocery shopping to restock his kitchen. Maybe he'd just grab some takeout from the local deli and take a sandwich by the hospital for Suzanne. At least that would be one woman happy to see him.

His thoughts circled back to Layla and the unexpected way she'd greeted him today. What was the emotion that had flashed in those hazel eyes of hers? If he didn't know better, he might have said fear, but that was ridiculous. Layla Dempsey had been fearless as an adolescent. She'd swung from the same rope into the creek as the boys and she knew how to ride a horse bareback. Hell, Jace had been more nervous about her losing her virginity than she'd been. He'd worried about hurting her, but the blissful smile she'd given him afterward had made him feel like a god.

He used to wonder, if he hadn't gone away to college afterward and she hadn't moved out of town with her father, would they have—

Knock it off. The Dempsey family was going through hell right now. It was Jace's job to be there for his friends, not to fantasize about Layla. All things considered, it was for the best that she'd turned down his dinner offer. And if he told himself that enough times, maybe the disappointment would fade.

Chapter 4

Time to face the dragon. Layla took a deep breath, trying to forcibly relax her posture in the driver's seat. Addie was already exasperated from the fifteen-minute drive to her grandmother's house and sitting still before that while Layla braided her hair. If her daughter picked up on Layla's tension, this was going to be a disaster.

Or, more accurately, an even bigger disaster than it was already destined to be.

Pasting a fake smile across her face, Layla put the car in Park and met Addie's gaze in the rearview mirror. "Ready to go see Grandma?"

Her daughter wrinkled her nose. "Do we hafta?"

A different parent might reprimand the girl for her petulant attitude, but that would be wildly hypocritical under the circumstances. "We won't be here long, baby."

Layla unbuckled her seat belt and went around the

side of the car to open the door for her daughter. Was she doing a good job with Addie Rose? Or would there come a day when her own flesh and blood would dread being in her presence? She hated imagining that her daughter might ever feel the way Layla did right at this moment.

As far back as Layla could remember, her mother had been disappointed in her. After first having a son, Claire had apparently looked forward to dressing Layla in pink and having tea parties with her and teaching her about makeup someday. But Layla had worshipped her big brother and wanted to do everything he did. She'd never understood why *she* got in trouble at the church picnic for getting her dress dirty when the only thing their mom said about Chris's torn slacks was *boys will be boys*. Still, despite their opposing viewpoints on how a young lady should behave, Layla had believed her mother loved her.

That changed when she was seventeen, panicked and pregnant, and chose to leave town with her father. Her parents' divorce had been brutally ugly; before it was all over, her dad hadn't just admitted to affairs, he'd rubbed them in Claire's face. The indignity of Layla *siding with him* had been the final nail in the coffin of an uneasy mother-daughter bond.

Layla hadn't been taking sides; she'd merely wanted to get as far from Cupid's Bow as possible before anyone learned she was expecting. It had also occurred to her that given her father's affairs and the shameful way he'd acted, he wouldn't have much moral high ground to lecture *her*. So she'd waited a few weeks and told him that she'd made a mistake at a party, trying to act cool so the kids at her new school would like her and getting carried away with a boy she didn't even know. Her dad hadn't been happy, but it was her mother who'd gone into full nuclear meltdown. There was probably still residual radiation around the house and yard. As she rang the doorbell, Layla slid a glance toward the rosebushes, trying to decide if any of them looked like mutant plants. There weren't any two-headed geckos sunning themselves on the front porch, so that was a good sign.

The door swung open, and there was Claire Brewer, her tight-lipped expression one Layla knew well. With the exception of a few more silver strands in her hair and less formal attire, she looked exactly the way she had at Chris and Suzanne's wedding.

Chris and Suzanne. Layla mentally chanted their names like a mantra, reminding herself why she was in town. Chris was close to their mother, and he didn't need any extra stress worrying about his family right now. For his sake, Layla would work to keep the peace.

"Hi, Mom."

"Layla." Claire's glacial tone thawed slightly when she glanced downward. "Addison."

"I'm Addie," the girl corrected. "Or Addie Rose. Or Pickle—that's what Grandpa calls me."

Uh-oh. Layla held her breath, wondering how Claire would react to mention of her hated ex-husband. They hadn't been in the same room since the day their divorce was finalized.

But Claire only cocked her head, her expression bemused. "Does he really? We used to have a cat named Pickle."

"I don't remember that," Layla said.

"It was before you were born, back when he and I were first…" Claire blinked, then squared her shoulders. "Come inside, won't you? The neighbors will wonder what happened to my manners if I make you stand on the porch all morning."

Worrying about other people's opinions—just like old times. In the final trimester of her pregnancy, Layla had been terrified of the upcoming birth. She'd begged her mom to come visit and give maternal advice, but Claire had refused, ranting about how her daughter had embarrassed the family. *Everyone in Cupid's Bow must think I raised a floozy! How am I supposed to hold up my head in public? Did you ever stop to think about that, young lady?*

It was difficult to forgive her mother for not being there when Layla had needed her most. If there was a silver lining, it was that she'd grown much closer to her dad; he'd doted on Addie from the moment he first held her in the hospital. Maybe he hadn't been a faithful husband or a very involved father, but he was trying to atone by being the world's best grandpa. It was a shame he didn't have that same opportunity with Chris and Suzanne's twins.

Addie marched inside, looking around with a critical eye. "Do you have a basement?"

Claire raised an eyebrow. "That's an odd question."

"Basements are the best place to go during tornados."

Layla patted her daughter's shoulder. "It's okay, Addie. I'm pretty sure there won't be any tornados today, so we don't have to worry."

"What if there's one tomorrow?" Addie asked. "She doesn't have a basement!"

"This is a very strange conversation," Claire said.

Layla pinned her mother with a warning glare. Addie was sensitive. Layla wasn't going to let anyone throw around words like *odd* and *strange* that made her daughter feel like a misfit. When a girl in her kindergarten class called her a weirdo, Addie had cried all afternoon.

"There's nothing odd about her being concerned for a relative's safety," Layla said. "It's sweet, when you think about it." *You certainly haven't given her much reason to care what happens to you.* Beyond annual calls on Christmas and Addie's birthday, Claire didn't interact much with her granddaughter.

"Uncle Chris got hurt," Addie said suddenly.

Claire's face softened, her eyes glinting with worry and unshed tears. Layla felt an unexpected tug of kinship, mother to mother. Did anything make a woman more vulnerable than fear for her child?

"Yes," Claire agreed. "He was very badly hurt."

"Does *his* house have a basement?" There was no logical link between tornados and being trampled by a bull, but Addie obviously equated basements with keeping her loved ones safe. Layla wanted to scoop her daughter into a hug. Too many people saw the girl's idiosyncrasies while overlooking what a big heart she had.

"No, he—" Claire stopped when the little girl's lip trembled. "You know what? He has a walk-in pantry that's down a few stairs from the kitchen. It's practically the same thing as a basement."

Addie craned her head around, looking to her mom for confirmation. Layla nodded. With that settled, Addie turned back to her grandmother. "Do you have a DVD player? I'm going to watch *The Wizard of Oz.*"

Claire shot Layla a chiding look over Addie's head. "With the witch and the tornado? Is that really such a good idea? It seems to me that—"

"Mom. Please let her use the DVD player." *And trust me to know what's best for my own daughter.*

"All right. I'll put in the movie. If you'll pour us some lemonade, Layla, we can take it on the back porch." Claire's steely tone was more command than suggestion.

Biting back a sigh, Layla headed for the kitchen. At least if her mom was about to lecture her she was doing it out of Addie's earshot. Did that count as progress? After Layla had set two glasses of lemonade on the porch table, she slid the screened door closed but left the glass one open so that she could hear if Addie needed her.

A moment later, Claire joined her on the patio. Surprisingly, she didn't launch into one of her tirades. Instead, she took a seat, not even looking at Layla yet. The silence was as chilly and tart as the lemonade.

I should say something. Layla wanted to reach out, but she was paralyzed by the memory of the last time she'd tried that, only to be rejected.

Claire stared out at the yard. "You're good with her."

"Th-thank you." Layla was so shocked by the compliment that a gentle breeze could have knocked her out of her chair.

"I suppose you don't think I was a good mother."

That felt like a trap. Still, now that Layla had some parenting experience of her own, she knew that being a mom was hard while making mistakes was easy. Motherhood was a minefield of potentially terrible decisions.

"Well." Claire's voice sounded tired. "I guess that answers that question."

"No, Mom, I was just trying to think of what to—"

Claire held up a hand. "I know I was…emotional during the divorce. I wasn't the steadiest parent. But, Layla, I don't think you understand how much that man hurt me. *Humiliated* me. I didn't mean to lash out at you, but for you to choose that bastard over your own mother…"

"It wasn't like that. I wasn't trying to choose anyone. I just wanted to get out of Cupid's Bow." That much was the honest truth. "I was going through a difficult time, too."

"So you tried to run away from your problems. But you're a grown woman now. I think it's time for you to come home."

"What?" Lemonade sloshed over the rim of her glass as Layla set it on the table with a thud. She had a life in Austin. Maybe not much of a social life, as busy as she stayed with work and her daughter, but she had clients and a professional reputation. This was Addie's first year of school. She was making friends and had a teacher who was patiently encouraging. Layla would need substantial reasons to rip her child away from her familiar routines and start over elsewhere. "Why would I do that?"

"What you mean, why? Cupid's Bow is your home. Your family is here. Don't you want to be there for Chris after all he's been through? Don't you want to see your nieces grow up? I'm sure Addie would enjoy spending time with them once they get a little older."

Layla resented the attempt to manipulate her through her daughter. "You barely know Addie!"

"And whose fault is that? How is it fair that the man who all but destroyed my life gets to see her daily while I—"

"*No.* You can blame Dad all you want for being a cheat and a liar—that's between the two of you—but he has nothing to do with the distance between you and me." Layla balled her fingers into fists to keep her hands from shaking, but she couldn't stop the tremble in her voice. "You could have been in the room when Addie was born. I called you, Mom. I cried, I pleaded.

I *wanted* you there. Your grudge was more important than your child."

"What a very convenient way to simplify my pain and paint me as the villain."

Layla shot to her feet. "Coming here was a bad idea."

There was no way in hell she would ever move back to Cupid's Bow. The way she felt right now, it would be a miracle if she even stayed in town the rest of the day.

Jace was walking up the sidewalk to Claire Brewer's front door when he heard snatches of an argument. He paused, realizing the raised voices were coming from the backyard. Apparently, Gena had been right to worry.

He'd stopped by the bank with a deposit from the store, and Gena had told him Layla was at Claire's. She'd been concerned about how the mother-daughter reunion might go, so Jace had manufactured a reason to stop by, hoping to lend Layla some moral support. He'd felt a little silly as he'd pulled into the driveway, uninvited, but now he knew he'd made the right call.

He went through the gate to the backyard, calling out a louder than normal hello to be heard above Claire's comment about "ungrateful daughters" and Layla's retort about "selfish mothers."

Both women spun toward him, neither looking happy to see him. Claire's face flushed red, while Layla's eyes widened to the size of poker chips. Her mouth dropped open.

Claire recovered first. "Jace. How…nice to see you. This is unexpected."

He held up the white deli bag. "I heard you were trying to stave off a cold, so I brought you some chicken soup. Thought you could heat it up for lunch."

She took it from him. "That's certainly thoughtful of you." The pointed way she cut her gaze toward Layla on *thoughtful* wasn't lost on him. He regretted being used to score a point in whatever fight they'd been having, but at least he'd gained Layla a momentary cease-fire. "I'll go put this inside. Thank you, Jace." She turned and stalked toward the house without another word to her daughter.

Layla covered her face with her hands, and he suddenly found himself at her side as if he'd been pulled there by a high-powered magnet.

He squeezed her shoulder. "Whatever she said to you, whatever she said *about* you… You have to know she's under a lot of stress. She probably hasn't slept for more than an hour at a time since Chris's fall. Don't let her make you feel bad about yourself, Layla—you're a remarkable woman." Until recently, he'd barely felt responsible enough to take care of himself, yet somehow she'd been managing a kid on her own, and, at twenty-four, was already a small business owner. Chris, proud big brother that he was, had shown Jace the website for her photography studio. She had a real gift.

Layla dropped her arms to her sides, her gaze troubled. "Remarkable? Oh, God, Jace, I'm really not. You don't…"

When her voice broke, a small piece of his heart did, too. He didn't know what to say, but maybe words weren't called for here. Acting on instinct, he enveloped her in a tight hug. He'd watched his brothers with their wives enough to know that the people you cared about didn't need you to have all the answers, they just needed to know you were on their side.

Although she didn't put her arms around him, she did melt into the embrace, burying her head against his shoulder. Was he a jerk for noticing how good she smelled?

"Stop being nice to me." She muttered the words into his sleeve, so at first he wasn't sure he'd heard correctly.

He drew back just enough to meet her eyes. "Did you ask me not to be nice?"

"I don't deserve it."

"Nonsense. You're—" Brave. Beautiful. Talented. And so close they could share breaths. His gaze dropped to her mouth and he suddenly remembered why he'd planned to avoid being alone with her. His heart pounded, sending desire through his veins.

"Jace." Her voice was low and husky, so sexy he almost groaned. "I... We..."

"Yeah." He had no idea what he was agreeing to; he was too focused on her lips, imagining them against his.

She cupped his face with her hands, leaning almost imperceptibly forward. He threaded his fingers through the wild waves of her hair and—

"Mama?" A little girl's voice came through the screen door, the owner of that voice mostly obscured by the floor-to-ceiling curtain.

Under normal circumstances, Layla shouldn't be able to knock a cowboy with Jace's height and weight advantage off-balance. But he hadn't been prepared for her to suddenly shove him away.

"Ow." He absently rubbed the hip he'd banged against the porch railing, but what really hurt was his pride.

"Coming!" Layla called, moving between him and the door. "Go wait in the living room, and I'll be in to restart the DVD." Her eyes flew to Jace. "You shouldn't be here."

That wasn't the impression she'd given him two minutes ago. Was she scandalized by the idea of her kid catching her mom kissing a man? That might suggest Layla didn't date often. The thought was oddly cheering.

"The store can spare me for a few more minutes," Jace said. "I can wait while you start her DVD, and then—"

"No, you need to leave. Now."

He had that same unsettling feeling he'd had at the hospital, that Layla Dempsey was afraid of him. A horrible thought struck. "Did I hurt you?"

She blinked. "What? I'm the one who knocked you over."

"No, not now. When we were teenagers. When we… It was your first time, and I tried to be gentle, but it's not like I was an expert."

"What do you think you're doing?" She dropped her voice to a frantic whisper. "We are so not discussing that! Especially not here."

"That's not an answer."

"No, of course you didn't hurt me. You were—"

"Mom?" The voice from the other side of the door held a note for impatience this time.

Layla moved farther away from him. "I have family stuff to deal with."

"Maybe I could hel—"

"Go. Away." Then she disappeared inside, the curtains swishing as she pulled the glass door along its track. It slid shut with a decisive click.

"Whatever the lady wants," he grumbled.

When they were teenagers, what she'd wanted was *him*. Clearly, times had changed.

Chapter 5

Saint that she was, Gena had taken off a second consecutive afternoon from the bank to help with Addie.
Today, they were thinking of even inviting over Skyler,
the six-year-old down the street, so that Addie might
make a friend. After waving goodbye to her daughter
and cousin—and sending up a prayer of gratitude that
they were getting along so well—Layla drove to the
hospital. She hoped that the time in the car alone would
allow her to regain her composure after a tumultuous
morning.

Instead, it just gave her way too much time to think
about Jace Trent. He'd almost kissed her! Or, worse,
she'd almost kissed *him*. What had she been thinking?

Maybe being a sucker for those blue eyes and his
touch was a case of old habits dying hard. After all, he
had been her first love. Truth be told, he might be the

only man she'd ever loved. *That wasn't love, Layla. It was adolescent infatuation. Grow up.*

She parked and went into the hospital, determined to stop thinking about him. But when she passed through the waiting area on her brother's floor, the first thing she saw was a couple kissing passionately by the vending machine. Their enthusiasm for each other took her straight back to that moment on her mother's back porch, and wondering what kissing Jace would be like now.

Blushing, she averted her gaze and tried to pass the couple as discreetly as possible, but the wooden heels of her mules were noticeably loud across the tile floor.

"Oh, sorry."

At the sound of a woman's sheepish voice, Layla looked up, meeting the eyes of a pretty redhead.

"We thought we were alone," the woman said. "Obviously."

For the first time, Layla realized who the woman had been kissing—Jarrett Ross. "Busted," Layla teased him. She turned back to the woman. "You must be Sierra."

The redhead nodded.

Jarrett draped an arm across his wife's shoulders. "Layla, this my better half—"

"Your much, *much* better half," Sierra said impishly.

He chuckled. "She was just, ah, saying goodbye before getting back to work. And, Sierra, this is Layla Dempsey. Chris's sister."

Sierra's smile faded as she reached forward to take Layla's hand in both of hers. "I am so sorry about what happened to your brother. As soon as he's ready for physical therapy, I will do my best to help him recover. And in the meantime, if there's anything Jarrett or I can do for your family, just let us know."

"Actually, there might be something." As Layla began outlining her plan for a fund-raising calendar, Sierra's and Jarrett's instant agreement boosted her confidence. The idea began to take real shape, distracting her from the stress of arguing with her mother. Unfortunately, talking about shirtless cowboys did nothing to distract her from Jace, but one problem at a time.

She was a professional. If he decided to pose for the calendar, she would focus on lighting and angles—*not* the play of muscles in his toned forearms. Or how damn good it had felt when he'd held her in those arms a few hours ago.

"Layla?" Jarrett gave her a look of concern. "Did we lose you?"

She blinked, realizing she'd trailed off midsentence. "Sorry. I was preoccupied."

Sierra nodded sympathetically. "This calendar project would be a lot of work for you. I imagine it's a little daunting."

Calendar. Right. She wasn't at all daunted by the thought of a certain sexy cowboy on the other side of her camera lens.

Layla tried to smile, but it felt strained, her cheeks stiff and uncooperative. "I just hope I know what I'm doing. Let's not tell Suzanne or Chris about this yet, okay? If everything goes the way I hope, it will be a lovely surprise for them. But at least we aren't getting their hopes up for nothing if it doesn't pan out."

"We'll get everything worked out," Jarrett said. "I remember how scared I was after my sister's accident and Dad's heart attack. Friends and neighbors rallied around my family. You may have been gone a few years, but you're still one of us. People will line up to lend a hand."

Too bad one of those people was Jace. He needed to keep his hands to himself. And she needed to find the discipline to do the same.

"Thanks for coming over, man." Will Trent clapped Jace on the shoulder. "I ain't gonna lie—being outnumbered three to one can get a little intimidating."

Jace chuckled. "Is the big strong fireman afraid of little girls?"

His older brother shrugged, refusing to take the bait. "I don't want to let Megan down. She's never left me with them for this long before. I figured the girls might be getting tired of my company, so having you here—"

He didn't have a chance to finish his sentence before a trio of identical dark-haired girls came running to the foyer. Cries of "Uncle Jace!" were bittersweet music. Jace adored his sister-in-law's daughters, but he couldn't help wondering again when he might have a family of his own. Being the tagalong bachelor uncle on the periphery of his brothers' lives had grown stale.

Daisy, the boldest of the triplets, reached him first. She threw her arms around his legs in a hug nearly powerful enough to topple him. It made him think back to the morning, when Layla had almost knocked him on his ass. Frankly, he'd been feeling off-kilter since the moment he first saw her yesterday at the hospital.

Will peered at him with concern. "You aren't getting sick, are you? If so, I retract my invitation. Megan and her aunt don't get back from their cruise until the day after tomorrow, and I am not prepared to take care of three kids with the flu."

"I'm fine." Jace scooped Lily off her feet for a hug. She was the shyest among her more outgoing sisters.

Although Jace had never been shy a day in his life, he knew what it was like to have siblings who always went full steam ahead. Lily was secretly his favorite, but he loved all three girls. He had ever since the December when Will had coerced him into playing Santa for the triplets. Jace had barely been in the house for five minutes before they'd won him over.

Too bad Layla hadn't introduced him to *her* little girl. He was great with kids. Would that impress her?

"You don't look fine," Will said as they herded the girls into a living room strewn with toys. Judging by the army of stuffed animals and plastic pink cups, Jace had interrupted a hell of a tea party. "Still upset about Kelli?"

"Who's Kelli?" Daisy demanded.

"Uncle Jace's friend," Will said. "You met her a few times."

"She had yellow hair," Iris told her sister.

"No, that was Jenny," Will said. "Kelli was—"

"Could we skip the instant replay of my social life?" Jace asked. "I'm going to the kitchen for beer."

"Get me one, too," Will said. "I'm sure it pairs well with these cookies." He held up a tiny yellow plate with nothing on it. "Iris made them special for us."

Jace grinned at the imaginary cookies. "I bet they're tasty *and* low-calorie." He went to the kitchen, surprised when his brother followed him.

"Seriously," Will asked in a low voice, "are you okay? You seem not yourself. Subdued."

"I'm just feeling…" Jace popped open a can of beer, searching for the right word. "Introspective."

"Who are you, and what have you done with my brother?"

Jace rolled his eyes. "People change, you know. They

grow." Was that part of Layla's confusing aloofness toward him? Did she still view him as the cocky teenager he'd once been? There was more to him than that now.

Then again, she hadn't exactly disapproved of him when they were younger.

He'd been stunned when she'd told him in a trembling but firm tone that she wanted him. He wished he could discuss her with Will, but no one knew about the night they'd shared. Though she hadn't technically sworn him to secrecy, telling anyone would feel like betraying her.

"I bet this is because of Chris," Will mused. "Seeing your best friend go through something that could have killed him made you take stock of your life. Is that it?" Without waiting for a response, he asked, "How's he doing?"

"About as well as can be expected. He's making jokes to keep Suzanne from worrying too much." Jace took a swig of his beer. "His sister's in town."

"Little Layla?" Will's smile was nostalgic. "You were too much of a self-absorbed punk to notice, but that girl had a wicked crush on you."

Jace almost choked. "Wh-what? Why do you say that?" The truth was, Jace *hadn't* noticed...until the night she'd pointed it out to him in no uncertain terms.

"Well, for starters—"

"Daddy! Uncle Jace! Your cookies are getting cold," Daisy scolded from the edge of the living room.

"Duty calls," Will said, turning toward his stepdaughter.

"But you didn't answer my question!" Jace winced at the edge of urgency in his tone.

Will must have heard it, too. He glanced over his

shoulder, eyebrows raised. "Does it matter? That was a long time ago."

"You're right." Jace forced a smile. "That's ancient history." Except for nearly kissing her today. That was very much in the present. And possibly also the foreseeable future. He wouldn't forget that moment when she'd leaned forward, soft and yearning, any time soon.

Of course, she'd shoved him away five seconds later with no explanation, as if he were something appalling.

Women. Jace chugged more beer and joined his brother in the living room. He wasn't sure how effective imaginary cookies were as comfort food, but they'd have to do until he came up with a better plan for the situation.

"I can't even believe you have to ask. Of course I'm in!" Quincy slapped a palm on the cafeteria table, looking delighted. "Shirtless pictures of me will not only pay your brother's medical bills—we might earn enough to put your nieces through college."

Layla laughed. "Thanks. I figured I could count on you."

"Absolutely. In fact…" Quincy winked at her. "I think we could ditch the other dudes completely. I have enough range to do twelve different poses."

"That wouldn't be fair to the ladies of Cupid's Bow—we have to give them the occasional month off from you to let them catch their breath."

Chuckling, he reached for his coffee mug and took a sip.

"So who all have you confirmed for this project?" he asked. "Me, Hugh, Jarrett—"

"Am I interrupting?" Jace asked from behind her.

Layla's heart sank. She wasn't naive enough to think she could have avoided him forever, but she'd hoped for a little more time to build her defenses after yesterday. If he touched her again, she was going to melt like a dropped ice cream cone in the Texas sun.

Jace pulled a chair from another table, swinging it around and straddling it. "Hugh told me y'all were down here, said Layla had something she needed to discuss with me."

Dammit, Hugh. But she knew her friend had been trying to help. She took a deep breath. "I might have an idea of a way we could all work together to raise money for Chris and Suzanne."

"It's an awesome idea," Quincy said. "We're banking on my sex appeal."

Jace arched an eyebrow. "Is this some kind of bachelor auction thing? We've had those in Cupid's Bow before. Funny story—it's actually how my brother Cole ended up married."

"Nah, not another auction. Layla's gonna put her photography skills to good use." Quincy checked his watch and stood. "I need to skedaddle, but call me, boo. Just tell me where and when you want me, and I'm all yours." He dropped a quick kiss atop Layla's head and ambled out of the hospital cafeteria.

She turned to catch Jace scowling after his friend. "What's wrong?" she asked.

"That man is an unrepentant flirt."

She blinked at the hypocrisy of his statement. "Um... look in a mirror lately?"

He held her gaze, those brilliant blue eyes making her stomach somersault. "I don't flirt with just anyone. I've grown out of that habit."

Was he trying to tell her that what happened yesterday was an uncommon occurrence? That she was somehow special? A long-dormant wistfulness tried to reignite, the idea that Jace Trent might truly want *her*.

She cleared her throat. "I suppose we've both changed, haven't we? I'm not the same girl I was." Translation—*I don't still dream about you every night and doodle "Mrs. Jace Trent" on spiral notebooks.* If she thought about him more often than was usual for a woman to dwell on a teen crush, well, who could blame her? Ever since she'd given birth to Addie, she spent each day looking at a reflection of Jace's eyes and smile.

"So what's this photography project?"

"A calendar. A cowboy calendar we can sell to raise money, using some of Chris's friends as models."

He took a moment to process that, then nodded. "Great idea. Women will buy the calendar for obvious reasons, and quite a few of the men in town will buy copies just to heckle us. If my brother Will posed for a calendar like that, there would be copies tacked up everywhere at the fire station within a week."

"So you're volunteering." It wasn't so much a question as grim acceptance of the inevitable.

"Of course. You weren't afraid I would say no, were you?"

Afraid? More like praying. "I..."

He gave her a wolfish smile that made her stomach do another slow flip. "When do we get started?"

Chapter 6

"How about I order us pizza tonight?" Layla offered when Gena got home from work Friday evening. Buying dinner was the least she could to thank her cousin for all her help the past few days. "I should probably volunteer to cook, but—" She gestured toward the papers littering Gena's kitchen table. She'd been sketching notes all afternoon while Addie played educational games on Layla's laptop.

Gena laughed. "You look like you're planning a battle. All you're missing are those little men to move around to show troop locations."

Layla tucked the pen she'd been using behind her ear. "Well, in my case, those pieces would be shirtless men in cowboy hats and boots. Do you know Grayson Cox?"

Her cousin nodded. "He's *hot*. But he only has eyes

for the town librarian. Lucky girl. You got him to agree
to the calendar?"

"Jace did. He left me a voice mail about it earlier."
She'd yet to decide whether dodging his calls was cow-
ardice or prudence.

Gena pulled a bottle of wine out of the fridge and held
it up in question. At Layla's nod, she pulled two glasses
out of the cabinet. A moment later, she joined Layla at
the table, passing her a glass of chilled chardonnay. "So
what's with all of the notes, General Dempsey?"

"Storyboarding." Her mind was racing with details
she needed to organize. "I have five guys lined up to
model. Both Washington brothers, Jarrett, Grayson and
Jace." Did her cousin notice how Layla's voice faltered
on his name?

But Gena was busy fanning herself. "Quite a lineup.
Are you trying to find seven more?"

"Nope. I figure I do one black-and-white shot and
one color shot of each guy, plus a black-and-white and
full-color group photo. That gets me all twelve months.
Dad is driving some of my equipment down to me—"

"Uncle Martin is setting foot in Cupid's Bow? Isn't
that like…opening an apocalyptic seal or something?"

Layla bit the inside of her lip. "Maybe my mother
won't find out?"

"Oh, honey." Gena leaned her chair back on two legs
to retrieve the bottle of chardonnay from the counter,
then splashed more wine in both of their glasses.

"I know, I know. But he offered, and I hate the thought
of shipping my equipment." Her photography gear was
the basis of her livelihood. "And even though I doubt
Chris will want to see him, I think Dad would feel better just being closer. You didn't see how wrecked he was

when we found out about Chris's injuries." Chris may have disowned their father in the wake of his scandalous affairs and bad behavior, but Martin Dempsey still loved his only son.

"Aunt Claire is going to—" Gena stopped abruptly when Addie skipped into the room.

"I finished all my counting games." She shifted from foot to foot, bouncing back and forth between topics just as quickly. "Hi, Cousin Gena. I like spelling games better. Is it dinner yet? I'm hungry. Did you have a good day with people's money?"

Gena grinned at the unorthodox description of her job. "I did, thanks."

"I want to do weather stuff when I grow up," Addie said, "but maybe a bank would be okay, too."

"It has its moments. Your mom was just telling me we might order pizza for dinner. Does that sound good?"

With a whoop of glee, Addie spun in a circle. "Pineapple and olives!"

Gena's smile was dubious. "I think I'll just go with boring old pepperoni on my half."

Layla nodded. She didn't personally share her daughter's taste in pizza toppings. Still, it had been a huge relief when Addie outgrew her phase where she would only eat foods in certain color groups. Parenting was such a guessing game. It was difficult to say which of Addie's behaviors were temporary and would dissipate over time and which ones might be more serious symptoms of an underlying problem. At the parent-teacher conference a couple of weeks ago, Addie's kindergarten teacher had broached the subject of maybe taking Addie to occupational therapy this summer.

Certain things helped—the twinkle jar, Layla rubbing

her back, rocking motions. When Mrs. Gainer pointed out how much Addie loved the playground swings and the child-sized rocking chair in the reading corner, Layla had purchased a padded glider for her daughter's room. Back home, Layla would wake up some mornings to find her daughter sleeping there instead of her bed. Heart squeezing with love and worry, she studied her daughter's face. There was nothing better than seeing Addie like this—smiling and enthusiastic instead of pensive or agitated.

Layla reached for her cell phone. "Gena, do you have the number for a place that delivers around here?"

An hour later, all three of them were stuffed full of pizza, and Layla had returned to her notes while Addie brushed her teeth and put on pajamas. That usually took a while, since Addie's ritual was to lay out all of her pajamas on the bed and evaluate each choice carefully. On nights when Layla was exhausted and wished she could get her daughter to sleep faster, she wondered if she should just buy Addie seven pairs of the same pj's.

"Printing costs and locations are next on my list," she said, thinking aloud while Gena rinsed their glasses at the sink. "Wardrobe isn't a problem. All the guys have their own variety of jeans and hats. But I don't want twelve photos set in the same place. I need to mix it up a little."

"Well, Jarrett owns a ranch," Gena reminded her. "You can probably find half a dozen picturesque spots on the Twisted R. Or... I don't know if there are rules against using the town park, but you could ask Mayor Johnston just to be sure. Jace's sister-in-law Kate has a family farm, out around Whippoorwill Creek, I think."

Layla jotted down the suggestions in questionable

shorthand that she may or may not be able to decipher later. She thought about texting Jace to ask for his sister-in-law's number—and to thank him for enlisting his business partner. No matter how much Jace triggered her flight response, she had to admit it was useful to have his support.

She set down her pen. "I can call Jarrett and Kate. But for the printing donations, I should really make my requests in person." She reasoned that it was more difficult to turn someone down face-to-face.

"The bank's only open until noon on Saturday," Gena said. "So I'm happy to hang out with Addie tomorrow afternoon."

"You're the best." Layla spared a grateful smile in her cousin's direction before reverting her attention to the list of tasks in front of her. "You know, the more people who know about this project, the greater the chance that Chris and Suzanne will find out. I hope people in Cupid's Bow know how to keep a secret."

Gena's laugh was wry. "It's possible you don't remember how Cupid's Bow works. But don't think of it as risking your secret, think of it as free word-of-mouth advertising for your product."

Risking my secret. A chill went through her. Could she and her daughter stay in town a couple more weeks without exposing Layla's biggest secret? She was probably being paranoid. Maybe no one would ever put it together who Addie's father was. Yet every time she looked at Jace, her apprehension escalated. Would he hate her if he learned the truth? Her heart thudded against her ribs like a trapped bird seeking escape. "Gena, I…"

"Yeah? What is it?"

Layla shook her head. It scared her to even say the

words out loud, as if Jace might hear them from the other side of town. "I just really appreciate all you've done. Letting us stay here, bonding with Addie, not disowning me when I stupidly got pregnant at seventeen."

"There's no one in our family who hasn't made mistakes. Ostracizing you for yours is total hypocrisy. You know I love you, no matter what."

"Even if, say, I lied about something?"

"You're my best friend. If you told a lie, I would assume you had a good reason." Gena pointed a finger at her, her expression comically stern. "Just promise me you'll never rob the bank. You could get me fired."

Layla laughed. "That, I can promise."

"Then, no matter what happens, I've got your back."

"Remember that when Dad gets to town and my mother goes nuclear."

"Good point." Gena grabbed the pen off the table and leaned over to jot a final item on Layla's to-do list. *Start building bomb shelter.* "Things are about to get interesting around here."

"Layla?"

She froze in her tracks, nearly tripping on the sidewalk. Shading her eyes against the sun, she glanced over her shoulder. "Jace."

"What a coincidence running into you." The mischief in his tone made it clear this was no coincidence.

"Are you stalking me?" That was all she needed on top of the last two frustrating hours.

"Since when is running into an old friend on Main Street stalking?"

"Who told you where I was? Gena?" She'd seen Chris

earlier, but she certainly hadn't mentioned her plans to her brother. "One of the business owners I visited?"

His lips quirked in a teasing half grin. "I don't remember you being this paranoid when we were younger."

Only since I found out I was pregnant with your child. She swallowed hard. "Well, great seeing you, but I have a lot—"

"I'm here to help."

She wanted to groan. He was the person she least wanted to see, yet every time she turned around, there he was. Literally. "You've already done so much. Agreeing to be in the calendar, recruiting Grayson, asking Kate about the use of her aunt's farm…"

His expression turned uncharacteristically serious. "Chris is my best friend. He's just as important to me as my brothers. Let me help him by helping you."

Even if she could manufacture a logical excuse for saying no, it would be impossible to resist the plea in his gaze. "Okay. I've been canvassing the area to see what kind of help I can get with printing costs. Maybe if we split up—"

"Actually, I have some thoughts on that I'd like to discuss. How 'bout I buy you a milk shake and we brainstorm?" He nodded down the street to the diner where he and Chris used to hang out after Friday night football games. The same diner where Jace had bought her dozens of strawberry milk shakes during her parents' divorce. The same diner where he'd found her crying in a corner booth after her first boyfriend dumped her when she was fifteen. *Any guy stupid enough to break up with you ain't worth the tears, beautiful.*

She shook away the memories. "A milk shake? I'm not a teenager anymore."

"No, ma'am." His eyes trailed over her in slow appraisal that sent heat rippling through her. "You are all woman."

With her rising temperature and suddenly dry throat, a milk shake didn't sound like a bad idea after all. "Jace…"

He took a step closer. "Yeah?"

She inhaled deeply, breathing in the familiar scent of sunshine and soap and denim. She had to ball her hands into fists at her sides to keep from reaching for him. "I appreciate all you're doing. But if we're going to work together on the calendar project, I can't—*we* can't— Dammit, you know what I'm trying to say."

"Not really." His eyes crinkled at the corners as he smiled. "Does it have something to do with the obvious sparks between us? Or how you almost kissed me the other day?"

"*I* almost kissed *you*?" She lowered her voice when a trio of women came out of the florist shop a few feet away. "I don't know what you're talking about."

He tapped his index finger lightly against her bottom lip. "You want me bad."

She whirled around and stalked toward the diner without bothering to answer—because he clearly didn't want to listen to reason, *not* because his words were true. He walked behind her, whistling cheerfully, and she might have pushed him off the curb into oncoming traffic except that there was no traffic.

Besides, she didn't entirely trust herself to touch him. She clenched her jaw, annoyed with them both. *You are a grown woman. Act like it.* The days of her getting all flustered because he flashed a dimpled grin at her were long gone.

He reached past her to open the door of the diner, and she studiously did not look at the sculpted forearms revealed by the sleeves he'd rolled up. "Ladies first."

"Thanks," she mumbled.

The mingled scents of sizzling bacon and freshly baked apple pie greeted her like an old friend. The diner looked exactly the same as it had throughout her adolescence. The robin's-egg-blue booths had been patched and the pictures of local kids' sports teams on the wall were more recent than the ones that had hung there a decade ago, but there hadn't been any real redecorating. No surprise there—Cupid's Bow had always been slow to embrace change. She was pretty sure the George Strait song playing on the jukebox was one she'd heard on her last visit here.

The vivid déjà vu conjured all the teenage nights she'd spent sighing over Jace, wanting him to feel the same way about her. Now he was following so closely that she could feel the heat from his body, and she wanted to stretch and luxuriate in it like a cat in a sunbeam. Figuring she'd be able to concentrate better once she had a table between them, she darted into the nearest available booth. He slid in across from her.

She glared, silently daring him to make any more outrageously flirtatious remarks.

Mercifully, his demeanor was businesslike. "Gena gave me the list of people you planned to talk to about printing today."

"A-ha! So she *did* tell you where I was."

"Of course she did." He shrugged. "I asked, she told. Neither of us thought your location was a state secret. Unfortunately, the top people on your list are the least likely to help. Mr. Barton only moved to town in the last few years. He doesn't have real history with the locals. He barely knows you or Chris. Mona Stapleton frets to everyone that she can barely make ends meet now that more average citizens can do their own design and printing on home computers. And Fred Chadwick… Well, he's just a jerk."

"That seems about right." Chadwick had all but chased Layla out of his store before she could finish a sentence. Mona, on the other hand, had been apologetic but firm. "Do you think we'd have any chance convincing Mona that the calendar would be good promotion for her? Less an unprofitable donation and more like free advertising?"

Before he could answer, a dark-haired waitress in a blue uniform came over to take their orders. The young woman blushed when Jace smiled at her, a feeling Layla knew all too well. How often had she looked at him with a similarly adoring gaze when she was sixteen?

"Two strawberry milk shakes," he said. Glancing away from his admirer, he asked Layla, "Do you still dip French fries in your milk shake?"

Only when no one was looking. "No, I outgrew that." Jace had stared at her in shock the first time he'd seen her do it, but she liked the sweet-and-salty combination.

"Uh-huh. And a side of fries to split," he told the waitress. Once the girl turned toward the kitchen, he shook his head at Layla. "So, is this like a lifestyle choice with you now? Denying what you want?"

"Well that's melodramatic. I just don't happen to be in the mood for fries."

"You're a terrible liar."

I'm better than you think. She cleared her throat. "So, about Mona…"

"You may be right—there's a chance we could persuade her to look at it as a promotional investment."

"Especially if you ask her." The words were out of Layla's mouth before she could think better of them. But their waitress was hardly alone in her open admiration of Jace.

He arched an eyebrow. "Meaning?"

"Just that you're…a Trent. Your family is very well respected around here."

Folding his arms across his chest, he leaned back in the booth, smirking.

"Okay, fine, you egomaniac. I meant that you're not unattractive and sometimes women respond to that." She wished she had a French fry within reach; she needed something to throw at him. "I'll bet you could persuade Mona."

"As I recall, you're pretty damn persuasive yourself." His voice was low, intimate. "Convincing enough to drive a man out of his head."

Layla's heart stopped. Did he think about that night often? She'd hardly been an experienced seductress, but the combination of pent-up longing and Jace's kisses had made her brazen.

"Here y'all are." The waitress plopped a plate of fries in the middle of the table. Then she set their milk shakes in front of them.

Layla grabbed hers and held the fluted glass to the side of her face, trying to cool her burning cheeks.

Jace eyed her for a long moment before redirecting the subject. "There's another option for getting the calendars printed. We ask Mona to do it at a discount and ask the townspeople to chip in for the difference. Grayson's girlfriend, Hadley, works at the town library, and it's not uncommon for her to put out a jar with an explanation about who needs help with what. It's low-pressure and unobtrusive. She doesn't try to browbeat anyone into giving, but the information is there for those who might be interested."

Layla bit her bottom lip. "If we post signs in the library or anywhere else around town, Chris and Suzanne will definitely find out about this before we even know if the project has been a success. More important, the townspeople are the target consumers. I'm counting on them to buy the finished product. It doesn't seem fair to ask them to finance the product in the first place, then turn around and charge them again."

"Okay, plan B, then. It was just bad luck that the people who make the most sense to do the printing aren't the business owners most likely to help you. Your brother's gone to the same barber his entire life, for example, and I'm sure Lavon would love to help—but he's not a great contact for a high-volume printing job. So how about we mix and match in the form of sponsorships? You mentioned a calendar as a promotional opportunity. What if, on the back, we thank the business owners who made the calendar possible? Mona, obviously, for providing the discount and labor, and a handful of other people carefully chosen by you and me. We can ask discreetly, without posting signs all over town."

"That's actually a really good idea!"

He chuckled. "Don't sound so surprised."

"No, I just meant… This is the first time all afternoon I've felt like things might come together the way I envisioned and generate enough money to be worth everyone's trouble." She grabbed a fry and happily dunked it in her shake. Cold strawberry ice cream dripped down her bottom lip, and she caught it with her tongue. When she looked up, she found Jace's eyes locked on her, blazing with blue flame.

"Outside earlier? When I joked about you wanting me? I was projecting," he said hoarsely. "I want you, Layla."

There was a time she would have walked across the state barefoot to hear those words from him. Her pulse raced, and she couldn't deny that part of her reaction was answering desire. But the stronger part was fear. She needed to keep her distance. "Jace, I told you, we can't… Things have changed. I'm not a reckless seventeen-year-old anymore. I'm a mother now."

"Are you suggesting women with children can't have sexual needs? Your logic is flawed, beautiful. Pretty sure sex is how people end up with children in the first pl—"

An involuntary whimper of distress escaped her, a small, strangled sound that couldn't possibly encompass all of her guilt and panic.

"Layla?" He frowned in concern. Then he paled. "Oh, God."

The dawning suspicion in his expression made her feel as powerless and nauseated as if she were watching a car accident happen. *No no no no*. Her lungs constricted. For a split second, she thought she might pass out.

"How old is she, exactly? How old is your daughter?"

She *wished* she could pass out. The oblivion of unconsciousness would be a blessing right now. The sweetness of strawberries in the back of her throat suddenly tasted like every nightmare she'd ever had.

Jace shook his head in denial even as his eyes narrowed in accusation. "She's not…mine, is she? I sound ridiculous. Of course she's not! You would have told me."

"I'm sorry." Tears began to spill over her cheeks. "Jace, I am so, so sorry." Then she was out of the booth, nearly crashing into a waitress.

Layla bolted for the exit, surprised but grateful that he didn't try to stop her. Maybe he was too shocked to follow. Or maybe he was just disgusted by the sight of her and wanted her gone. She wouldn't blame him. At the moment, the only thing stronger than Layla's own self-disgust was the soul-deep need to protect her daughter from whatever came next.

Chapter 7

Growing up, Jace had never done as well in school as his older brothers. It had been embarrassing to struggle in classes all day, then be surrounded by straight-A students at the dinner table each night. But he'd never felt truly stupid until right this moment, staring sightlessly after Layla while he sat anchored by the enormity of the truth.

How could I not have guessed before now? He'd taken the virginity of a teenage girl and hadn't stopped to do the math when he later learned she'd had a baby? So. Damn. Stupid.

Then again, he'd been nineteen and striking out on his own for the first time, self-absorbed with his life. And Layla's family hadn't exactly advertised her pregnant-and-unwed status. He struggled to recall when he'd first heard she was a mother. Had someone in his family told him, or had it been Chris? Had his best friend known this entire time about Layla's secret? The betrayal already knifing through him sharpened until common sense kicked in—if Chris found out Jace slept with his sister, there would have been a violent reckoning years ago. So Jace wasn't the only one she'd kept in the dark.

The biggest reason it had never dawned on him to question whether he was a father was the simplest: he'd trusted her. They had been friends. He'd known Layla her entire life, and he'd cared about her. He'd never imagined that she might lie to him. Even now, in the wake of her unspoken confession, part of him still rejected the possibility of her being dishonest. How could she have kept his own child from him? He was a *father*. Yet he'd missed first steps and first words. He knew nothing at all about his daughter. Was she artistic like his niece Aly, or shy like Lily, or athletic like—

My family! Thoughts of his brothers' children made Jace realize the scope of the situation. Not only was he a dad, Cole and Will were uncles. Jace's parents had a new grandchild they hadn't even known existed. His mind reeled. Did he call a family meeting or tell each of them individually? Over the phone or in person? Who should he talk to first?

The tiny corner of his brain that was still able to function rationally whispered *Layla. You have to talk to her before you do anything else.*

But he couldn't. Not yet. The rage and hurt were too raw. He might say something that would destroy their friendship forever. *So what? She's not your friend. She's a liar.*

Her apology echoed in his head, but he refused to be

swayed by the ragged heartbreak in her voice. *Jace, I am so, so sorry.* Ha! Sorry she got caught, maybe. Would she ever have told him the truth if the guilt on her face hadn't given her away? He imagined his daughter learning to drive at sixteen without him there to share pointers. Walking down the aisle on her wedding day without him beside her.

Blind with fury, he reached in his wallet and threw a handful of bills on the table, overpaying and not caring. He sure as hell hoped one of his brothers had sage advice on how to forgive Layla because, right now, he didn't trust himself to speak to her ever again. He would have to, though, in order to meet his daughter. Layla had kept them apart far too long, and he'd be damned if he would sit on the sidelines of his child's life.

Time to start making up for lost years, whether Layla Dempsey liked it or not.

The sun was setting when Layla finally staggered through the back door of Gena's house. After she'd made it to her car earlier, she'd driven to the nearby park and had a long cry. It had taken over an hour to get it out of her system. She'd finally been calm enough to drive to her cousin's, but now she was dehydrated and exhausted.

"Hey." Gena greeted her from a bent-over position, checking on whatever was cooking in the oven. "You're back in time for dinner. Did Jace find you? He— Dear God. What happened?" Tossing a polka-dotted oven mitt on the counter, she regarded Layla with alarm.

Layla knew her eyes were swollen and her face was tear-stained. "Where's Addie?" The last thing her anxious daughter needed was to see Layla ravaged with grief.

"I asked her to wash up for supper. Are you okay? Did something happen to Chris? Is—"

"No, it's not that. I'll run Addie a bubble bath later, and we can talk then. You two start dinner without me. I'm not hungry, anyway. I'll just go…" *Second-guess my entire adult life? Wish today had never happened?* "Splash some cold water on my face." Yeah, that would solve her problems.

Gena squeezed her hand. "Whatever it is, things will be okay. You're a survivor, Layla."

Maybe. But survivors could still be bad people.

She would never forget the look on Jace's face as he tried to reason himself out of the truth. *She's not mine. You would have told me.* As a terrified teenager, Layla had impulsively done what she thought necessary to survive the crisis and start a new life for her and her daughter. She'd succeeded, but at what cost? What would the fallout be from the choices she'd made?

The scared, reactionary part of her wanted to put Addie in the car and put Cupid's Bow in her rearview mirror. *You can't keep running away.* It had worked once—temporarily—but she wasn't seventeen anymore. And consequences had a way of catching up.

"You know," Cole drawled as Jace rolled down his truck window, "this is the kind of behavior I arrest people for. Wanna tell me why you're parked outside my house in the middle of the night like a thief casing the place?"

"Middle of the night? It's barely dark."

"Which doesn't actually answer the question." Cole frowned. "I don't know what's up, but come inside. We'll talk about it."

That was exactly why Jace had come here—to share everything that had happened with his big brother and get Cole's advice. Yet, when he'd tried to imagine what to say, where to begin, he'd been so paralyzed with conflicting emotions, he hadn't even made it out of the truck. "I appreciate the offer, but I'm not fit company."

"That's never stopped you before."

"Ha ha."

Cole rounded the front of the truck, then got in on the passenger side. "Last time I parked with someone in a truck on a dark street was senior year with Bobbi Sue McClain. You are a serious step down from that."

Jace rolled his eyes. "If Bobbi Sue walked by you on the street in a bikini, you'd be too busy doting on your wife to even notice."

"Very true." Cole grinned the self-satisfied smile of a man completely content with his life. It would be obnoxious as hell if it weren't so genuine. "Kate and the kids are my world."

Jace hated how jealous the statement made him. Kate and Cole were partners. They shared everything—affection, children, inside jokes. Kate would never have lied to her husband. *Yeah, but Layla's not your wife. She wasn't even your girlfriend. She was just a kid.* Why was he trying to rationalize her actions? She'd kept the truth from him—for *years*. "What if Kate did something you couldn't forgive?"

"What are you talking about?"

"I'm mad at…a friend." The word stuck to the roof of his mouth like peanut butter. Friends didn't betray each other. "I'm trying to figure out how to move past it."

"As the sheriff, I can't endorse this, but speaking as your brother, have you considered just taking a swing at him and then buying a beer? That seems to work for the Breelan brothers when they need to solve disputes."

"This friend is female."

"Oh. Forget what I said about taking a swing." Cole was quiet a moment, processing. "Is this Kelli? Are the two of you talking again?"

"No. Doesn't matter who it is."

"The hell it doesn't. Your hypothetical comparison was Kate. You didn't ask how I'd forgive one of the deputies at the station or one of my poker buddies who ticked me off. You asked about the woman I love. What's going on, Jace?"

Words and phrases ricocheted around his mind. He hesitated, unsure who he was trying to protect—Layla or himself. As angry was he was with her, he didn't want his family to hate her. And there was no way to explain that she'd had his child without first admitting he'd slept with his best friend's teenage sister.

Even though he'd been a teenager, too, he should have had the good sense to send her away. Her feelings would have been hurt, but she would have recovered. Cole was going to smack him upside the head for giving in to selfish temptation *and* for not bothering with a condom. No matter what assurances Layla had made at the time, Jace should have taken some responsibility. An extra minute or two of effort on his part would have changed everything for her. She wouldn't have left Cupid's Bow, pregnant and ashamed. There wouldn't be a rift between her and her mother. Ever since she'd fled the diner, he'd been furious with Layla, but some of his anger was beginning to shift direction like a weather vane in the wind. He'd gotten her pregnant and permanently altered the course of her life. It was a miracle she didn't hate his guts.

Cole cleared his throat. "You're starting to freak me out a little. What's with the skulking outside my house and the weird mysterious silences?"

"I'm just realizing that some things are difficult to discuss." If he, a grown-ass man, was having trouble telling his brother about this, how much harder had it been for her as a kid to face her family?

"Are you sure you don't want to come inside?" Cole pressed. "Luke is at a friend's house, but the girls are home. You know they always love seeing you."

Not too long ago, Jace had decided that, as much as he loved being an uncle, he was ready to be a dad. Now he would find out the hard way whether he'd been right. Was he ready? Would interacting with his own child come as naturally to him as the hours he'd spent playing and joking with his nieces? Or would he botch it up somehow? There would be a new level of pressure he'd never experienced.

"Actually," Jace said, "I think I'm gonna head home for the night. Think some things over."

"Okay. You know where to find me if you change your mind." Giving him one last curious look, Cole climbed down from the truck and headed inside to his family.

Once Jace made it back to his own place, he fired up his laptop. Moments later, he was on the website for Layla's photo studio. She had a gallery of pictures so that potential clients could see her work. No names were listed of the subjects, but there was one little girl shown in a variety of shots at a few different ages. She was the curly-haired miniature of her mama. His heart twisted, but not just with pain and betrayal. This time there was something sweet and sharp, too. *I'm a daddy.* He enlarged the photo. On the screen, his daughter stared back with eyes surprisingly like his own, and Jace knew he would never be the same.

"Oh, wow." It was the fifth time Gena had said that in as many minutes. She seemed stuck on repeat. "I just… Wow."

"I know." Layla sniffled, reaching for the tissue box her cousin had set on the kitchen table. "It's a lot to process."

"And your parents don't even know?"

Layla shook her head. "You're the only one who knows." Jace's appalled expression flashed through her mind. "Well, you're the only one I've told, anyway."

"Do you want wine?" Gena stood. "I feel like I should pour you wine."

"Thanks, but I'm majorly dehydrated. Wine would just make my headache worse."

Her cousin sat back down. "I wish I knew what to say."

"At least you're speaking to me." Despite the many negative emotions Layla had experienced in the last twelve hours, now that she'd finally told someone the whole story from start to finish, she actually felt a tiny bit better.

"I cannot believe your first time was with Jace Trent. Lucky girl."

"Gena! That's so not the point of all this."

"I'm surprised you didn't tell me back then what you planned to do."

"I almost did, but I was afraid you'd try to talk me

out of it—which would have worked. I was nervous as hell. I didn't know what I was doing."

"Clearly. Or you would have paid more attention to the birth control instructions." The teasing gleam in her eyes faded. "What about Addie? What have you told her about her father?"

"The truth, more or less—that he was someone I loved but that he lives far away now and that we were separated before he knew she was in my tummy." She squirmed in her chair, aware that she was stretching the boundaries of honesty. Austin and Cupid's Bow weren't that far apart. "It hasn't come up much yet. Kids adjust to whatever norm they're raised with. She never had a dad, just me and her grandpa, and she didn't voice much curiosity about it until this year, when she started school. Even now, there are kids in her class with one parent, three parents, same-gender parents… I don't think the lack of a father has traumatized her too much."

"You trying to convince me of that or yourself?" Gena asked gently.

Layla turned in the direction of the bathroom, where they could hear the faint sounds of Addie splashing and singing in the tub. For all her anxieties and phobias, she'd never been one of those kids who was nervous about swimming pools or water. "I love her so much."

"I know you do. Which is why you have to tell her about her dad. You'll need to come clean with your mom and Chris, too."

"Oh, God." She covered her eyes with her hands.

"Jace and his family are close. He's probably already told them." Gena glanced out the window, as if checking for an angry horde of Trents with pitchforks and torches.

"You can't risk that Chris or Aunt Claire—or, God forbid, Addie—will hear the truth from anyone but you."

Layla heaved a sigh. "The reason I came to town was to help Chris. He doesn't need the stress of this news. What if it drives a wedge between him and Jace? Or what if my mother comes unhinged, and my brother gets more preoccupied with mediating than recovering?" Now that the truth was beginning to leak out, she owed the people in her life some explanations, but wouldn't it be better to at least wait until Chris was out of the hospital? "Do you really think Jace has told his family already?"

"Hard to say." Gena gave her a sympathetic look. "But there is one person who knows for sure."

"What am I doing here?" Layla muttered as she waited to see if there was a response to her knock. "I should have just called." She'd considered phoning, but she'd decided there was a better-than-even chance that Jace would hang up on her. It was much more difficult to get rid of a determined woman with her foot wedged in the doorway.

The front door swung open, and Jace stood there in a dark blue T-shirt and Dallas Cowboy sweatpants. If he was surprised to see her, he didn't let it show in his guarded expression.

"I know it's late," she said apologetically, "but I didn't think you'd be asleep. Under the circumstances."

"Good guess."

She tensed, braced for anger and accusations.

But then he sighed, stepping out onto the porch with her. "I get why you're here—we definitely need to talk—but I don't think I can do this tonight."

"I understand." She leaned on the railing, reliving

old memories and the crushing sense of being so over-whelmed she could barely breathe. "When I first suspected I might be pregnant, I drove two towns away to buy the test. When it turned up positive, I was so… I couldn't think. I was scared and numb and dazed. I got in so much trouble that week because I couldn't concentrate on a thing my teachers or my mom said to me. I was putting my shoes on the wrong feet and bumping into walls. It's a miracle I didn't accidentally wander into traffic. So I know what it's like to need time to process."

"Layla, I'm sorry."

She blinked. "*You're* sorry?"

"That you went through all of that by yourself. Cole and his wife had another kid a little over a year ago. They were thrilled, but Kate was so sick during that pregnancy. And midway through, one of her test results came back wonky. There were a couple of scary weeks when they thought something might be wrong with the baby. When I think about you facing all of that while I was away at college, sleeping through lectures, changing my mind about my major and hitting on sorority girls…"

"I don't need the details."

He shoved a hand through his hair, and she had an ill-timed recollection of running her own fingers through it. "I'm older than you—"

"By less than two years."

"—and I was the only one of us with actual sexual experience. If I'd just bothered with a condom—"

"Then I wouldn't have the most precious person in my life." She locked gazes with him, needing him to understand that she'd never once regretted having their daughter. "Jace, the last few years haven't been easy, but I wouldn't trade them for anything. Addie Rose is…"

It should be easy to tell him about Addison. Every time another parent came into the studio, Layla ended up sharing anecdotes about Addie. But now it felt like a monumental task, as if she had to find the exact perfect words to encapsulate her bright, sensitive, complicated child. Words weren't enough.

She sat on the top step, patting the space next to her as she pulled her smartphone out of her pocket with her other hand. Tapping the screen, she opened the album labelled Addie. "Here." There were over one hundred photos. When it came to pictures, she was a digital hoarder.

He sat down next to her, looking wary. "What's this?"

"Your…" She swallowed the lump in her throat. "*Our* daughter."

When he took the phone from her, his hand brushed hers. It was ludicrous that something so small could cause goose bumps, but a mere touch of Jace's fingertips was still inexplicably potent. The light from her phone cast a glow on his face, and she watched him as he swiped through moments of Addie's life. There weren't any baby pictures on the phone, but Layla had kept her favorites from the past two or three years.

"She's beautiful," he said hoarsely. He glanced her way for the briefest of moments before looking back at the screen. "She looks like you."

"She has your eyes."

The corner of his mouth lifted. "I noticed that earlier. I…looked up photos of her in the gallery on your website."

That admission sliced through her. Jace Trent was a good man. He deserved so much more than a few dozen digital images. Still, it wasn't as if she could wake Addie up tomorrow with, "Guess what! You have a daddy now!" They had to approach this with Addie's best interests in mind.

She hesitated to ask questions she might not want the answers to, but forewarned was forearmed. "Have you... told anyone? About her? About us?"

He set the phone down between them, and her heart pounded with dread.

"Not yet," he said finally. "I went over to Cole's tonight. I value his opinion, and I wanted to vent to someone. But, for whatever reason, I just couldn't do it. It was too hard. Too much."

She nodded, recalling all the times she'd wanted to tell her family the truth. Until tonight with Gena, she'd never managed it.

"I'm angry with you, Layla. So freaking angry."

"I know."

"But...I don't want to be. Part of me understands."

Her eyes stung with emotion. Partial understanding was more than she deserved—which made it difficult to ask him for a favor. He didn't owe her a damn thing. "I know eventually we'll have to tell our families. But for now, do you think we can keep it between us? I'm not asking for myself, Jace, I swear. But for Addie. We have a lot to figure out before we explain the situation to her."

He studied her, but the phone had gone dim and she couldn't read his expression. "For now," he agreed. "It won't be the first time we've shared a secret, will it?"

Her body tingled in remembrance, and she wished she could kiss him. It wasn't the girlish desire she'd once felt. It was more like the impulse to seal some sort of pact. Or maybe it was meant to soothe away the pain she'd caused him today. Whatever her motivation, she found herself leaning closer. He met her halfway, his hand cupping the nape of her neck. Then his lips were moving against hers, and her toes curled.

Gone was the nineteen-year-old boy who'd once kissed her tentatively, as if half waiting for her to change her mind. Now, he devoured her. Her own conflicting feelings were echoed in his kiss. There was hunger and sorrow and joy. Even anger—he bit her bottom lip, the slight sting a contradiction to the gentle way he caressed her. He traced his fingers up the back of her neck and threaded them through her hair, tugging her closer.

He'd shifted so that he was nearly on top of her, and his muscular body pressing into her felt so good that she arched her back. And banged her head on the porch railing. When she winced, he pulled away, his expression sheepish.

"Guess I got carried away," he said.

She rubbed the base of her skull. "You weren't the only one." What in the hell was she thinking, practically jumping him in his front yard? Their situation was complex enough without adding lust to the mix. She stood, putting space between them. "We should both get a good night's sleep and talk during daylight hours." *Good luck—he'll be just as attractive then as he is in the moonlight.*

Jace rose, too. "Why don't you come back in the morning? I'll cook you breakfast."

"What? Here? Oh, I wouldn't want you to go to the trouble. I was thinking a restaurant." Surrounded by de facto chaperones.

His chuckle had an edge to it. "What's the matter, beautiful? Afraid you won't be able to keep your hands off me if we're alone?"

Yes. "Someone certainly has a sizable ego."

He winked at her. "Everything's bigger in Texas."

She couldn't believe, after everything, that he was flirting with her. When she'd driven over here, she hadn't even known if he would be speaking to her. When he turned on the charm, she melted inside. Apparently, her years away from Cupid's Bow had not made her immune to Jace Trent. Regardless, she had to make mature choices now; she couldn't behave like a lovestruck teenager.

Squaring her shoulders, she asked, "What time should I be here for breakfast?"

He'd been looking at this all wrong.

By the time Jace watched dawn streak the sky with yellow and pink, he had a whole new perspective. His eyes felt like he'd rubbed them with sandpaper, and he was keyed up from the coffee he'd been drinking for the past hour, but he was grinning from ear to ear. Yesterday, when he'd stumbled across the truth about Addie, he'd been shocked and outraged by Layla's secret. But if she'd come to him when he was nineteen and told him she was carrying his child, what would he have done? Panicked and fled to Mexico? Grudgingly married her to appease both of their families? He would have been a terrible husband and father. He'd been immature and unprepared for that kind of responsibility.

But now, *now*, he was ready. And life had dropped this amazing second chance in his lap. He'd been envying his brothers, wondering when he would have a wife and family of his own, only to discover that he had a child—and that her mama was a woman he'd known and cared about his entire life. He and Layla clearly had chemistry, as well as history together. If the reason she'd left Cupid's Bow was to keep her secret, it shouldn't be hard to convince her to come home. She had nothing to lose now. They were in this together.

He inhaled deeply, appreciating the sunrise through the kitchen window. *It's a brand-new day.*

And, soon, he would begin a brand-new chapter of his life. He couldn't wait for Layla to arrive, couldn't wait to tell her he'd forgiven her. He imagined her relief and joy, imagined her kissing him, smiling against his mouth. They could pick up where they'd left off last night, but on the much more comfortable king-size bed.

Ever since he'd encountered her at the hospital last week, he'd wanted her. At first, he'd tried to fight it, feeling like a traitorous friend to Chris, but the situation was different now. Given the circumstances, Chris would probably *want* them to be a couple—after a brief adjustment period, anyway.

Balanced on the balls of his feet, Jace rocked back and forth, debating whether to make another pot of coffee. It was too soon to start breakfast preparations. Too bad none of the stores in town opened this early. He had the urge to go buy the biggest teddy bear he could find. He was antsy to meet his daughter, to introduce her to her cousins. It couldn't be easy for a kid to only have one parent. Addie didn't know it yet, but she now had a dozen new family members who would love and support her once they learned of her existence. He hoped he could convince Layla to start telling people soon. It was everything he could do not to email his brothers links to Addie's pictures online.

He'd scrutinized the photos countless times throughout his sleepless night, trying to memorize and interpret his daughter's expressions. What had Layla done to make her laugh so hard in the picture from last autumn? Or did Addie just like playing in the leaves? In one shot, her smile had been sleepy, a faraway look in her eyes. It led him to wonder about her bedtime routine. Was she one of those kids who fought sleep, begging for just one more story or glass of water? Or was she like his friend Grayson's son who could fall asleep anytime and anywhere, including midsentence or facedown at the dinner table?

Yesterday, questions like those would have strangled Jace with bitterness. He'd been so hung up on the unfairness of not knowing his own child that he'd overlooked the sheer joy of *getting* to know her. He had so much to look forward to, so much to share with her. Did she already know how to swim? Had she ever been on a horse? He hadn't felt this much anticipation since his short-lived days in the rodeo ring.

He glanced at the digital clock above the stove, willing time to go faster.

As far back as he could remember, he'd been the odd one out in his overachieving family. He'd struggled to figure out who he was and what he wanted. Both of his brothers had pretty much selected their careers by kindergarten, but Jace had bounced between college majors before eventually dropping out. He'd tried his hand at a variety of jobs, and he'd dated scores of women. For perhaps the first time, he had a clear vision of what his life could be—and he wanted that life to start as soon as possible.

Chapter 8

Layla awoke with her daughter's toes jabbing her in the rib cage—not that she'd really been in a state deep enough to count as sleep, anyway.

When she'd returned from Jace's last night, Addie had been asleep. But around one in the morning, she'd climbed into Layla's bed, saying she'd had bad dreams. Layla had wrapped her arms around her daughter and contentedly breathed in the lavender scent of her no-tears shampoo. It had been a peaceful balm to her frazzled emotions...for about three minutes. Addie didn't just kick in her sleep, she performed Rockettes-caliber extravaganzas. Somehow, in the middle of the night, she'd ended up completely perpendicular to her mother, feet embedded in Layla's side.

After yesterday's crying jag, cracking her noggin on Jace's porch and a night of being kickboxed by her kid, Layla was in serious need of ibuprofen. Rubbing her bleary eyes, she tried to crawl out of the bed without disturbing her daughter more than necessary. As it was, she hadn't decided how to handle going to Jace's for breakfast. She might make it there and back before Addie woke. But there was an equal or greater chance that Addie would wake and be dismayed that Layla had left without saying goodbye or giving her an explanation. *What kind of explanation?* She didn't want to lie to her kid, but she couldn't tell her the truth, either. Not yet, and certainly not before coffee.

Mercifully, the aroma of fresh-brewed coffee was already beckoning from the kitchen. *Bless you, Gena.* Layla shambled down the hallway like a caffeine-seeking zombie in slippers and a robe.

Gena stood in front of the refrigerator in yellow-and-red-plaid pajamas, her hair in a curly ponytail, looking cuter than anyone had a right to before 8 o'clock.

"Isn't Sunday your day off?" Layla asked. "I figured you would sleep in."

"If only." Gena pulled out the low-fat creamer and shut the fridge door. "My internal clock is a heartless bitch. She doesn't give me days off. I assume you would like a mug of coffee, too?"

"Unless you have an IV handy. If not, I'll make do with a mug."

Gena chuckled. "You were awfully quiet when you snuck in last night. I didn't even realize you were back until after you'd gone to bed. How did it go?"

Well, Jace has become an even better kisser, which I didn't know was possible. But that probably wasn't what her cousin meant. "Better than I expected, but our conversation wasn't very in-depth. He needed more time. I'm actually headed over there for breakfast."

"That sounds promising. Amicable, cooperative."

Tempting. Layla still questioned the wisdom of being alone with him, but it would certainly be easier to keep a secret if they weren't discussing the situation within earshot of nosy neighbors. "I wish you could come with me. For moral support."

"Uh, pass. That would be unprecedented levels of awkward. Besides, you need me to stay with Addie."

Layla sipped her coffee, willing the caffeine to move faster on its trip to her brain cells. "I can't decide whether to let her sleep or wake her up to say goodbye. She doesn't do well with surprises." *So how on earth will she handle news of her father?* Layla's head throbbed even more as she thought about her daughter's nervous reactions to the unexpected, everything from upset stomachs to elaborate rituals.

"What if we split the difference?" Gena suggested. "Write her a quick note letting her know when you'll be back. I'll keep an eye on her and read the note with her as soon as she wakes up, so she doesn't have time to feel abandoned. If you think you're gonna be awhile, text me. Maybe I can take her and Skyler to a matinee. Think that might work?"

"Addie adores you, so as long as she wakes up in a positive frame of mind, it should. She was having nightmares last night. Poor kid's probably feeding off my stress," Layla said.

"Don't beat yourself up about it. You'll only stress yourself out more. Think mellow thoughts."

Easier said than done, with another visit to Jace's looming. What if he changed his mind about not telling anyone yet? What if he tried to kiss her again? What if, as someone who'd been raised by very involved parents, he pushed for some kind of custody arrangement where Addie stayed with him periodically? That would be a huge disruption to her routine. If Layla pointed that out to him, would he fight her on it?

By the time she parked her car in front of Jace's house, all the what-ifs were swirling in her aching head like one of the cyclones her daughter found so enthralling.

Layla pulled the keys from the ignition and studied the small house through the windshield, getting a better look at it than she had in the dark. Jace was renting his late grandmother's place from his parents, and the 1940s bungalow looked much the same as it had on the occasions Layla had visited as a child. Someone had repainted the exterior and replaced the old porch railings, but the rustic charm was the same. It suddenly struck her that Jace's grandmother was Addie's great-grandma; this house was part of her daughter's heritage. Her stomach churned at the thought of how disappointed the Trents were going to be in her.

She trudged up the porch steps, regretting the coffee she'd chugged. The caffeine was doing nothing to settle her stomach. Jace flung the door open so quickly that she jerked back, startled. Her pulse beat triple time. *Definitely no more caffeine.*

"You're here!" His smile was dazzling in the morning sunlight. Before she could answer, he had a hand at her waist and was propelling her inside. "Can I get you some coffee?"

"Um, I'll just have water." And antacids, if she could find any in her purse. She set the bag on an antique end table. The front room was dominated by a leather sofa set; the muted greens and rich browns of the area rug on the hardwood were masculine but welcoming. "This place looks a lot different. Nice, but different."

The corner of his mouth kicked up in a grin. "Fewer crocheted doilies and ceramic armadillos, right? Unlike Nana, I don't collect breakable knickknacks, and my furniture is pretty sturdy. It's kid-friendly—no confusing decorative soaps you aren't allowed to use or glass vases to break. If Cole's daughter Mandy hasn't destroyed anything by playing soccer in the house, I doubt Addie could cause any damage. Does she play sports?"

"She—"

"I wondered about horses, too, if she's been riding yet. Cole, Will and I had all been on horseback before we were school-age. Does she like animals?"

"Yes. To the animals. No to the horseback riding. And no to the sports." There'd been a short-lived attempt at soccer, but Addie had hated the way the required shin guards felt against her legs. Plus, she got far too upset if she didn't score a goal during a game, feeling she'd let her team down. Layla had reminded her that, while winning was nice, it was important to have fun, only to realize her daughter wasn't actually having any. "I was considering putting her in swim lessons this summer. She loves the water."

He looked delighted. "Cupid's Bow has an amazing aquatic complex. People come from all over neighboring counties to use it."

"I know, but…" His casual talk of Addie spending time in town, at his house, was unnerving.

"I hope you're hungry." Jace strode toward the kitchen, bustling with energy. Had he always been this much of a morning person? "I've got fruit and sausage ready and the batter mixed for pancakes. There's a bacon-and-cheese quiche in the oven."

"You know how to make quiche?"

"No, I know how to preheat the oven and open a box." He grinned over his shoulder. "But I hold my own at pancakes. I almost never burn more than half of them."

She smiled at that, the closest she'd come to relaxing since she'd arrived. Once she was seated at the table, however, watching him pour circles of batter onto the electric skillet, he resumed his inquiries about Addie. Yet he barely let Layla respond before thinking of something else he wanted to ask. He hurled questions at her with the speed of a major-league pitcher who had his heart set on the Cy Young Award. Trying to keep up hurt Layla's brain.

Did Addie prefer pancakes or waffles? Summer or winter? What was her favorite color? Was she a morning person or a night owl? Did she have a preferred bedtime story and did she already own a copy of *Where the Wild Things Are*?

He set two plates on the table, each full of enough food to feed a family of four. "Of course, my favorite story to read to my nieces is *The Book with No Pictures*. It teaches all-important vocabulary words like *blork* and *globbity*. What was Addie's first word? Does she use *grandma* and *grandpa* for your parents, or does she have sillier nicknames?" He cut into his pancake but paused with a bite halfway to his mouth, suddenly beaming. "What do you think she'll call *my* parents?"

"Jace!" She pressed her fingers to her temples, needing him to shut up a second so she could hear herself think. *Don't bite his head off.* "Slow down. You're... coming on too strong." If Layla was this overwhelmed by his rapid-fire interrogation, how on earth would Addie feel?

"I'm just eager to get to know my daughter."

"You're peppering me with trivia questions. Memorizing a handful of random facts about someone isn't the same as really knowing them."

His fork clattered onto his plate, his blue eyes stormy. "And whose fault is it that I never got the chance?" he asked softly. "That I don't even know my daughter's birthday?"

She sucked in a breath, struck by the truth in his words. He was right. Still, she had to protect her anxious daughter from his full-steam-ahead approach. Her conflicting guilt and maternal instincts made her head throb worse. "I need air." She scraped her chair back across the hardwood and made a beeline for the front door.

Jace was right on her heels. "You were never a coward when we were kids. This pattern of running away doesn't suit you. The diner yesterday, leaving Cupid's Bow—"

"I was seventeen." The cool morning air on her face was a relief after the warm confines of his kitchen. Her voice was slightly less shrill when she added, "And I was terrified."

After a long moment, he sighed. "And alone." He put a hand on her shoulder.

She stiffened, remembering too clearly their interlude on the porch last night, but she didn't resist when he gently spun her around into a hug.

"You didn't tell your family the truth and you didn't tell me, and you had to deal with it alone." He stroked a hand over her hair. "You aren't alone now."

She closed her eyes, indulging in how good he felt. When people bought the shirtless cowboy calendar, they would probably notice Jace's sex appeal, the hard muscular planes of his torso. Admittedly, he was a very sexy man. But right now what she appreciated most was the *solidness* of him. His chest beneath her cheek was irrationally reassuring, somehow making her feel as if the two of them were a team who could take on the world.

But temporary enthusiasm didn't necessarily translate into long-term partnership. Parenting was more than sunny days at the playground and silly bedtime books. It was also getting kicked in the ribs and sacrificing a good night's sleep and occasionally getting thrown up on and questioning whether your kid's quirks were normal or if you were making the mistake of not intervening soon enough. Layla cared about Jace Trent—she always had and she always would—but he had a habit of quitting when things got difficult or he lost interest.

She pulled away, replaying his words with different emphasis in her head—*You aren't alone* now. Sure, but what about next week or next year?

There were difficult decisions to be made when raising a child, and she didn't want to fall into the trap of relying on Jace's assistance to make them. She'd done her best by Addie for the last six years. She would continue doing so, with or without a man's help.

She looked out across the yard, still seeing in her mind's eye the tire swing that had once hung from the big oak tree, recalling games of tag with her brother and the Trents after one of Jace's birthday parties here. It was on the tip of her tongue to tell him when Addie's birthday was and that her favorite flavor of birthday cake was German chocolate. Instead she asked, "How long have you and Grayson been in business together?"

"Not too long. He bought back his father's old store

from one of his dad's ex-partners, then decided that running it by himself was cutting too much into his family time. So he started looking around for someone, and it just so happened I was between jobs. My parents cut me a good deal on renting this place, so I saved up more than you would think during my bartending days. It was one of those... What's that word for happy accidents and coincidences?"

"Serendipity?"

He snapped his fingers. "Exactly. Like you being back. I broke up with my last girlfriend because I wanted to have kids, a family. She didn't. And now here you are, telling me I *have* a kid. How often does life work out that perfectly?"

Never, in her experience. "Jace, my being in town isn't a *happy accident*. I'm here because my brother got trampled by a bull. And deciding to have kids isn't like having a craving for tacos. It's not an easily satisfied temporary whim. You should put real thought into it."

He gave her a pointed look.

"Okay," she relented. "Obviously I didn't make an informed decision to get pregnant. But as soon as I knew, I did think long and hard about whether it would be best for the baby for me to raise her or to give her up for adoption. I read books, I scoured internet forums on parenting, I even took a childcare course at the local rec center. And I was the only member of my Lamaze class there with her father, which was humiliating, but I was determined to make good choices for Addie. I still am. I want you to meet her, but before we tell her you're her long-lost daddy—"

"You say that like I went missing," he said flatly.

"Even during the years I didn't live here, you could have contacted me through my family or Chris."

"I know. I probably should have. I didn't want to disrupt your life, and I wasn't sure what was best for her." Her voice trembled. "Meeting strangers isn't easy for her. If Gena is okay with the idea, are you free to come over for dinner tonight? At least then, Addie will be in a setting where she already feels comfortable."

His expression brightened. "Tonight? I can meet her tonight?"

"As long as Gena says yes. Under the circumstances, I suspect she will."

"So she knows?" He didn't sound bothered by that. Quite the contrary, he sounded hopeful.

"She wanted to know why I'd been crying, and I made an exception by telling her. It's not like I'm ready to post an announcement in the *Cupid's Bow Clarion*."

He didn't seem to hear her. With an unrestrained whoop of glee, he lifted her off her feet and spun her in a circle. "Just text me what time to be there. Wild horses couldn't keep me away."

Yes, he was certainly giving her that impression. "Jace…" Would it be a waste of breath to caution him again about slowing down, about approaching the situation with restraint?

He met her gaze, correctly reading the concern there. "Quit worrying, beautiful. Uncle of seven, remember? I've got this."

She hoped he was right. For all their sakes.

"Thank you." Layla shot her cousin a sheepish smile across the kitchen. "I mean, I know I already said that—"

"Only two or three hundred times." Gena winked at her.

"Well, I'm really grateful." Layla turned her gaze back to the bread dough she was rolling into crescent shapes on the baking sheet, stifling the impulse to say thanks yet again. Or apologize again. "Oh, God. What if this is a disaster?"

"I'm sure it will be fine?"

Layla raised an eyebrow.

"Okay, I'm not *sure*. But what was it our mothers used to say? Don't borrow trouble?"

Mention of her mother did nothing to calm Layla's nerves. Her father would be arriving to his hotel on the outskirts of town tonight, and Layla still hadn't figured out how—or if—she should tell her mom or brother.

"My movie is starting again!" Addie's update came from the living room. "Does anyone wanna watch…or make popcorn?"

Gena chuckled at the unsubtle hint. "Want to go keep her company, and I'll get the rolls in the oven?"

Layla bit her lip. "Honestly, I have so much nervous energy, I'm not sure I could sit still." All she'd told Addie about tonight was that a friend was coming to dinner, someone who grew up with Layla, Gena and Chris. Aside from her usual scowl at the prospect of meeting a stranger, Addie had been unfazed. It was probably better that Layla keep a safe distance so that her tension didn't spill over onto her daughter.

"All right, I'll hang with the munchkin," Gena volunteered. "There might still be a line of dialogue in the first twenty minutes that I haven't memorized yet."

Layla laughed. When she and Addie left Cupid's Bow and went back home, Gena would probably be happy never to hear mention of *The Wizard of Oz* ever again. "You're the best."

"Very true."

Although Layla couldn't honestly say that she was looking forward to dinner, it was a relief when Jace pulled up to the wide gravel half circle that served as Gena's driveway. Getting this over with had to be better than torturing herself with imagined scenarios. She took a deep breath. *Here goes nothing.*

When she opened the door, she found herself staring at a colorful bouquet and a plush horse. "Um…" *Brilliant greeting, Layla.* After last night's ill-advised kiss, she wasn't sure how to interpret the flowers, but they made her nervous. Well, nervous*er.*

"Hey." Jace grinned from between the stuffed animal and some sunflowers. "Am I too early? I had to stop myself from driving over here half a dozen times. I was really excited."

"I see that." She stood aside, eyeing the floral arrangement. "You, ah, didn't have to bring me flowers."

"I didn't. These are for Gena, to thank her for having me over to dinner. My sister-in-law Megan is a florist, and I asked her to do something appropriate to hospitality." He shifted his feet, his gaze sliding to the stuffed horse cradled in his arm. "And this, of course, is for Addie."

His voice trembled slightly on their daughter's name, and Layla's heart squeezed. Jace might hide it behind charm, but he was nervous, too. This was a momentous occasion.

"Come on," she invited softly. "She's in the living room, watching one of her favorite movies."

"Is it about a princess?" He set the flowers on the

ledge of the half wall that marked the entryway. "Thanks to all my nieces, I know a lot of princess movies."

"Not a princess, just a Kansas farm girl." Since Layla was walking slightly in front of him, she didn't see Jace's expression when he got his first look at Addie cuddled against Gena on the plaid couch. But Layla heard the way his breathing stuttered. She couldn't help wondering what would have happened if she'd called him in his dorm room his freshman year of college and informed him he was going to be a father.

Clearing her throat, she grabbed the remote off the end table and pressed Pause. "Addie? There's someone here who would like to meet you. You remember Gena and I told you about our friend Jace?"

"Hello," Addie mumbled, dutiful enough to offer the greeting but shy enough that she didn't make eye contact.

Jace moved past Layla, nodding to Gena without taking his gaze off his daughter. "Hi, Addie. I brought you something." He held the horse out toward her.

"Why?" She scowled. "It's not my birthday."

"Oh, I…" He was obviously surprised by the question but recovered quickly. "It's just how I was raised. When I have dinner at other people's houses, I bring gifts for the people there. I brought Gena a bunch of flowers. They're in the other room."

"What did you bring Mommy?" Addie asked.

"Dessert," Layla said quickly. "He brought us a chocolate cake for after dinner." Her daughter didn't yet know about the bakery box in the refrigerator or that Mrs. Washington had given it to Layla at the hospital.

Jace changed the subject. "So, you like *Wizard of Oz*, huh?"

Addie nodded. "Have you seen it?"

"Not in a long time, but it's a good movie. I always thought the black-and-white part was a little boring, but once she lands in Oz and it's all colorful and everyone is singing, it gets pretty interesting."

Layla and Gena winced in unison. Calling his daughter's favorite part of the movie boring was not an auspicious start.

Addie's small face puckered in an expression of bewildered derision. "The beginning part has the *tornado*."

"Sure," Jace said, "but later, there's a talking scarecrow, a castle, flying monkeys—"

"Is anyone else really hungry?" Gena interrupted. "I am starving."

"Me, too," Layla said, even though she hadn't had an appetite all day. "Why don't we all go to the table? Maybe we can talk more about movies there."

But Addie didn't seem to hear them. She was frowning intently at Jace. "You were at Grandma Claire's. With Mommy."

Layla's stomach clenched as she recalled being in Jace's arms on her mother's back porch. Did Addie recognize his voice, or had she seen them together? And if so…how much had she seen? Injecting as much cheer into her voice as possible, Layla said, "Jace has known our family a long time. He brought Grandma Claire some soup for lunch while we were there the other day. And he's been friends with Uncle Chris ever since they were little boys."

"That's right," Jace said quickly. "Want to hear some funny stories about your uncle when he was a kid?"

Addie regarded him with suspicion. "I need to wash my hands for dinner." She climbed down from the couch, leaving the untouched toy horse behind, and left the room.

Jace heaved a sigh, and Layla watched her daughter go, wondering how to make this evening go smoothly.

"Well." Gena was the first to break the ensuing silence. "Would now be a good time to ask if anyone wants wine?"

The uneasy silence hanging over the dinner table might not have been so conspicuous if people were focused on enjoying their meals, but apparently Layla wasn't the only one without an appetite. Normally, Jace was never at a loss for words, but he was uncharacteristically hesitant, as if worried he'd say the wrong thing to Addie after his *Wizard of Oz* faux pas. Layla was mentally kicking herself for not doing a better job of prepping him, for sharing more of her daughter's likes and dislikes. She'd honestly intended to that morning, but he'd barely let her get in a word edgewise.

This is a fiasco.

Addie was regarding the adults around her with obvious suspicion, and Gena had just glanced toward the refrigerator as if considering a second glass of wine. If Layla brought any more chaos to her cousin's life, the poor woman was going to end up a lush. Or maybe Gena was just thinking about the chocolate cake in the fridge. If ever there was a time to bend the "no dessert unless you eat your veggies" rule, it was tonight.

"Is anyone else in the mood for chocolate?" Layla asked. "Maybe it's time to cut the cake."

Gena nodded emphatically. "Lord, yes."

Addie's suspicion only grew. "We're not allowed to have cake in the middle of dinner."

"I know," Layla agreed, "but sometimes on special occasions—"

"Why is it special?" Addie interrupted. She pointed at Jace. "Is he like Mister Kyle?"

"Kyle?" Jace looked to Layla for explanation.

Her cheeks heated. "Someone I dated. Briefly." Kyle had been the closest she'd come to having an actual boyfriend. Although he hadn't had kids of his own, he'd assured Layla that he wanted them someday. He'd been eager to meet Addie, but then he'd tried much too hard to win her over, making her uncomfortable. He'd alienated Addie and strained his relationship with Layla—until abruptly abandoning them for a pretty barista with a less complicated life.

Now Jace was scowling, and, under different circumstances, the fact that his expression was identical to Addie's might have been cute. The mention of Layla seeing someone obviously irritated him. Was he jealous of her romantic past, or was it the idea of another man spending time with Addie—time he'd been denied—that upset him?

"I don't want cake," Addie declared. "Can I go watch my movie instead?"

Layla bit her lip, caught between wanting to encourage her child to be polite to guests and knowing that sometimes letting Addie retreat was the best way to avoid a meltdown.

Jace took the choice out of Layla's hands. "Of course you can." His shoulders slumped, his posture one of defeat.

Giving him the closest thing to a smile she'd offered all evening, Addie scrambled out of her chair.

Gena was hot on the girl's heels. "I'll, uh, just see if she needs help with the DVD player." It was a flimsy excuse to leave them alone, considering Addie had mastered the remote days ago, but Layla appreciated her cousin's diplomacy.

Jace shoved a hand through his hair. "I guess I'll be going."

There were a lot of things Layla wanted to say, but she should probably make sure there was no chance of Addie overhearing. "Do you want to tell her goodbye first?"

"You tell her for me. I think she'd rather I not interrupt her movie again."

Layla couldn't honestly refute that. "I'll walk you out."

Neither of them spoke again until she'd closed the front door behind them. Was there any chance she could lighten the mood? "Well, you survived the first meeting. It's bound to get easier from here, right?"

He met her gaze, his complexion unnaturally sallow under the orange porch light. "We both know that's not true."

She'd never seen anyone more crestfallen. *This is my fault.* She'd impulsively thrown out the idea of dinner because she hadn't known what else to do, and none of them had been properly prepared. "Jace..."

"I just wanted her to like me."

She reached for him, the embrace half comfort and half apology. "She will. You just have to give her time."

Burying his face in Layla's hair, he tightened his hold on her. "God, I hope you're right."

It was jarring to see brash, confident Jace Trent so deflated. She rubbed circles on his back, the way she used to do for Addie when she couldn't fall asleep. "Hey, it's going to work out." It had to. Somehow. "You're very likable, remember?"

He pulled back just enough to peer down at her, scrutinizing her expression as if to decide whether she was telling the truth. After a second, the corner of his mouth twitched. It wasn't a smile, not by a long shot, but it was a start. "Yeah?"

"Yeah."

Their gazes held. She felt the subtle change in his bearing—an alertness. An undefinable energy. Answering energy buzzed through her system. He ran the pad of his thumb across her bottom lip.

She shivered. "Jace—"

"Please." His husky voice was cajoling, far more tempting than any chocolate cake on the planet. "It's been a difficult night. One kiss, beautiful, to make it all better?"

His logic was flawed. Rationally, she knew that. Far from fix anything, kissing Jace had the potential to make a complex situation even worse. But how could any woman resist a *please* from Jace Trent? Especially when she so badly wanted to indulge in the momentary refuge of pleasure. Logic and reason be damned. Inhaling a shaky breath, she stood on tiptoe as her eyelids fluttered closed.

But before either of them could do anything more, headlights cut across the yard. Layla sprang back as tires crunched over the gravel. Gena hadn't mentioned expecting anyone. Jace muttered a soft curse at the timing.

When the car parked and the headlights cut off, it took Layla's eyes a moment to readjust to the dark. The person climbing out of the car, however, was so familiar to her that she recognized him instantly. *"Dad?"*

"Mr. Dempsey?" Jace's tone was horrified, and Layla had a moment of déjà vu to the time her father had caught Jace and Chris with an adult magazine when they were thirteen or fourteen.

She stepped forward to meet her father—and to put more distance between herself and Jace. "Dad, what are you doing here? You were supposed to call me from the hotel and figure out plans, not just show up at Gena's."

Her father looked both sheepish and stubborn. "Is that any way to greet the man who drove your camera gizmos all the way out here?" He hugged her. "I missed you and the pickle. And I haven't seen Gena in a month of Sundays. So I thought I'd...surprise you."

His slight hesitation spoke volumes of vulnerability. He was estranged from his family. Had he worried that, given warning, Gena might refuse to see him? Layla's heart lurched. He'd made a lot of selfish mistakes in the past, but she had to believe in second chances and forgiveness. Otherwise, how could she ever forgive herself for not telling Jace the truth sooner?

Jace. Yikes—she was going to have to tell her father the whole story. Preferably when the man who'd gotten her pregnant as a teenager wasn't standing within ass-kicking distance.

She cleared her throat. "Dad, I'm sure you remember Jace Trent."

The two men nodded politely. Was she the only one who saw the wariness in Jace's expression? She gently shoved him in the general direction of his truck. "Nice to see you again. All our best to your family." To her father, she said, "You can go on inside. You'll find Addie watching *Wizard of Oz.*"

Her father's grin was a gleaming flash of teeth in the darkness. "Color me shocked. You, uh, sure it's okay if I just go in?" At her nod, he started toward the house, absently whistling "Somewhere Over the Rainbow" as he walked.

"So," Jace said, "she watches that movie a *lot*, huh?"

Layla was too busy trying to process the adrenaline that had flooded her system to answer him. Good Lord. She'd almost been busted making out with Jace Trent by her father! As mortifying as that would've been, it was not the worst-case scenario. What if *Addie* had seen them? She recalled the mutinous expression on her daughter's face when she'd demanded, *Is he like Mister Kyle?* Addie and Jace were already off to a rocky start. Layla couldn't believe she'd almost let hormones make the situation worse.

Keeping her voice down as her dad crossed the yard, she said, "That can't happen again."

"What?"

"You and me. And the kissing." Her skin heated just at the thought of it. He was really *such* an excellent kisser. Dammit. "It was probably never a good idea, but there's too much at stake now. You just got through telling me that you want Addie to like you. If she catches us together like that… It would be confusing for her."

He was quiet for a long moment, and she wondered if she'd offended him.

"Jace, you have to understand. I—"

"Has she seen you kiss many guys?"

Hardly. She could count on one hand the number of guys she'd been physical with since Addie was born. But was that any of his business? She knew good and well that Jace Trent hadn't been celibate for the last seven years. "Are you questioning my judgment as a mother?"

"No," he said softly. "Just trying to get a picture of what my daughter's life is like."

Touché. Suddenly his question didn't seem that unreasonable. What must it be like, trying to imagine Addie's life with no insight or frame of reference? "I think she's witnessed two kisses, and one was under the mistletoe at a neighborhood Christmas party. Which means watching us kiss would make you pretty damn memorable."

"I want to be."

"Well, sure, of course, but not for playing tonsil hockey with her mother."

He choked on a laugh. "You did not just say that."

"Oh, please. I heard you and Chris say much crasser things when I was young and impressionable."

"I guess that's true enough." Leaning against a tree, he hooked his thumbs in his front pockets, not meeting her eyes. "Don't you think there might come a time when she'll want to see you with a man? When she might want a father? Have you ever thought about who that man would be?"

The question stretched between them like a creaky suspension bridge over a cactus-filled gorge. Was he asking because he worried about another man taking the place that was rightfully his...or because he hoped there might someday be something romantic between the two of them? Something more than furtive kisses in dark yards.

Unable to formulate a response, she answered his question with a question. "Who knows what the future holds? But for now, we keep our hands to ourselves. Agreed?"

He made a noncommittal sound in his throat.

"I should get back inside. Gena hasn't seen my dad in years. They might need a buffer."

"If you say so." On the surface, his tone was polite enough. Neutral.

But she'd known Jace Trent since she was in preschool, and she heard the underlying taunt in his voice. He thought she was running away again. Well, to hell with what he thought—there was a perfectly good reason flight was an instinctive response that had been honed by evolution. Sometimes, it was the best way to survive a situation.

She lifted her chin, refusing to let Jace make her feel like a coward. Single moms were survivors by necessity. "Good night, Jace."

"I'll see you soon, beautiful."

A pleasant shiver brushed along her skin, and she told herself it was a result of the cool evening breeze. Sometimes, denial was a necessity, too.

Chapter 9

Jace was starting to have a real understanding of how rivers could carve out entire valleys. It had been thirty-six hours since he'd last seen Layla, and her words kept running through his head, gentle but relentless, eating away at all his other thoughts. *For now, we keep our hands to ourselves*. It was the *for now* that had him so preoccupied.

Even though he knew it was a bad idea to be distracted while behind the steering wheel, he couldn't stop thinking about her as he drove toward the Twisted R ranch—especially since he knew he'd see her there. Today was the first photo shoot. She'd verified by email that everyone could make it out to Jarrett's ranch and said that she wanted to get started with some group photos.

He hadn't really spoken to her since leaving Gena's the night before last. There'd only been the emails about

the calendar and a succinct text asking him not to tell
Chris yet that their father was in town. Not a problem.
Now that Jace knew *he* was the reason Layla spent her
senior year of high school pregnant, he was having trouble looking his best friend in the eye. He'd visited the
hospital yesterday while Chris was waiting for a doc-
tor to sign his discharge papers. Jace had spent most of
the time discussing college football and finding reasons
to leave the room frequently and fetch things for Chris
and Suzanne. The worst part was, even while he'd been
standing in his buddy's hospital room, analyzing Uni-
versity of Texas's coaching staff and repressing low-key
guilt, Jace had still been thinking about Layla.

For now, we keep our hands to ourselves. Okay—
for now. But what about later? Because he'd realized
something the other night. He wanted Layla Dempsey.
He'd told her as much at the diner; the sexual attraction
between them was no surprise. But this went deeper.

Watching her in such a domestic setting, interacting
with her child, *their* child, had done something to him.
Granted, the night hadn't gone all that well, from Addie
being unimpressed with his gift to Martin Dempsey
driving up as Jace was about to kiss Layla good-night.
Still, there had been moments that were like glimpses
into an alternate reality, one where he might be snuggled
on a couch with Layla and Addie or sharing conversation about their day over the dinner table. It was surprisingly simple to imagine being with her after a long
day at the store, weary after bad-tempered customers
or late shipments, and having it all melt away when he
took her in his arms. He didn't just want sex; he wanted
the rest of it, too.

How quickly could he convince her that she might

want that, too? Time was not on his side. It was wonderful that Chris had been released from the hospital, but with her brother slowly healing and this calendar project getting underway, how long did Jace have before she took his daughter and left him behind? His body tensed in a combination of urgency and dread. It wasn't until the *vroom* of the engine roared at him that he realized he was flooring the accelerator.

Easing his foot off the gas, he tried to think strategically. With the exception of Kelli leaving because she didn't envision the pitter-patter of feet in her near future, he'd never really had problems with his love life. But if he *had*, he would have turned to his older brothers for advice. He didn't know how to talk to them about any of this without revealing Layla's secret. Breaking his promise to her not to tell them yet wouldn't go very far in winning her over. So if—

"Crap." He blinked at the intersection ahead of him. *This isn't right.* Despite being out to the Twisted R hundreds of times, he'd gone the wrong way. Had he really missed a turn he should be able to find in his sleep because he'd been so preoccupied with a woman? Maybe it was best his brothers didn't know about this. They would mock him mercilessly.

Making a U-turn on the deserted road, he tried to banish Layla from his thoughts long enough to successfully reach the Ross family ranch. Judging by the assortment of trucks already parked on the grass, he was one of the last to arrive. He immediately scanned the area for Layla, but didn't see her or any of the guys.

"They're down by the barn," a female voice called.

He turned to see Sierra emerging from the main house, cute as a button in a plaid shirt obviously meant for Jarrett's much taller frame and a pair of jeans. She pulled a rolling cooler behind her.

"Hadley and I were just headed that way," Sierra added. Sure enough, the town librarian stepped out of the house a second later.

Hadley smiled. "Hey, stranger. Long time, no see."

She was kidding. She'd brought barbecue to the tack-and-supply store last night for Grayson's dinner, which Jace's business partner had graciously shared. Hearing Hadley tell Grayson all about the twins' afternoon had left Jace antsy to call Layla and ask about Addie's day. He'd resisted, though, giving her room to breathe and himself time to ponder options. When he'd gone to Gena's to meet his daughter, he'd shown up with more enthusiasm than consideration. Next time, he would do better.

He returned Hadley's smile. "Good to see you again. Boys with you today?"

She shook her head. "They're 'helping' Grayson's aunt do some yard work, which means she'll wear them out for us, but they'll be covered with mud when we go pick them up. It seemed wrong to bring children with me, considering."

"Considering?" Jace echoed.

"All of the ogling we plan to do," Sierra declared. "I invited our whole book club to watch the shoot."

Jace blinked, not sure if she was kidding.

"I wanted to sell tickets," Sierra said, "but I got voted down. Talk about a way to raise money…"

Laughing, Hadley elbowed her in the ribs. "I *meant* that I thought it would be a bad idea to have the boys underfoot around Layla's sophisticated photography equipment. You know the twins. I love them dearly, but they can break anything just by looking at it."

"So, there isn't really a book club congregated to watch the process?" Thank God.

"No." Sierra pouted comically. "But only because this calendar is supposed to be a secret. Otherwise, I would have set up makeshift bleachers and rented a margarita machine."

Hadley grinned. "Best book club meeting ever."

Jace shook his head at them. "Troublemakers."

"Through and through," Sierra agreed. "In lieu of margaritas, I suppose this more sensible cooler of cold sodas will have to do. If you want to take it down to the barn for us, we can go ahead and be on our way. We're meeting a friend for a chick flick. Jarrett says the theater in town is actually playing a movie from this year, miracle of miracles." She sighed longingly. "When I think about the cinemaplex in the city… There was one where they brought you cocktails! The seats were actual recliners with fully extending footrests and speakers built right into your chair."

"Seriously?" Hadley looked impressed.

Sierra pressed the back of her hand to her forehead like the tragic heroine in a terrible play. "The things I sacrificed to move to the middle of nowhere to be with Jarrett!"

Jace laughed. "Hadley, I don't know why you're paying good money to be entertained by a movie. This one's plenty of drama all by herself."

Sierra made a mock curtsy in acknowledgement and handed over the cooler of drinks.

As he approached the barn, Jace heard people talking. At first, it was just a rumble of masculine voices. He recognized his friends speaking but wasn't close enough yet to make out the specifics of what anyone said. But then Layla spoke, and it was as if his ears were finely tuned to pick out *her* voice. He heard her say that the pond was a good suggestion for a backdrop, but they'd have to contend with mosquitos. She made a joke about the calendar not selling well if her shirtless cowboys were covered in swollen red bugbites, although she supposed the local pharmacy could use them as ads to sell mosquito repellent. There was a ripple of laughter and even from a distance Jace found himself smiling.

His smile faded when he entered the barn. Hugh and Grayson were seated on bales of hay and Jarrett was on a weather-beaten chair in the corner, which he'd tilted back on two legs. Jarrett's shirt was partially unbuttoned, but the three of them were all dressed. Quincy Washington, however, was shirtless and standing entirely too close to Layla, grinning at her. Jace had the irrationally possessive urge to walk up and kiss her, to publicly stake a claim.

Yeah, try that and see how it goes, genius. She'd bash him over the head with a camera.

"Jace, you made it." Grayson Cox nodded toward him.

"Hey." Jace returned his partner's greeting, but his gaze kept sliding back to Layla and Quincy, the only other single man in the barn. It had been a few years since Jace participated in the rodeo. Were his arms still as toned as the other man's? Did Layla prefer men who were lean or bulked up with muscle?

That line of thinking was ridiculous. Jace had never worried about comparing himself to another man before. He'd grown up with older brothers half the girls in town swooned over, but that hadn't hurt Jace's social life any.

"All right," Layla said crisply. "We're all here, so we should get to work. I appreciate all of you for agreeing to do this and don't want to waste any of your time. Jace, we were talking about possible locations for pictures. I don't want twelve shots of pasture—"

"Pretty sure the ladies who buy the calendar won't be scrutinizing the backgrounds," Quincy teased.

Layla waved a hand. "Consider it a matter of artistic integrity. *Anyway.* I need a variety of settings. Taking some inside makes sense, but it feels a little claustrophobic for a group photo. I won't have as many angle options. So let's take this outside. We can get some great shots along the fence." Without waiting for agreement, she picked up a dark bag and exited the barn, her stride purposeful.

Jace grinned, reminded of a stern elementary school teacher and a field trip he'd once taken. *Come along, single file, this means you, Jace Trent!* He'd been disregarding the single-file rule in an attempt to hold hands with Anabelle Shermer.

Outside in the sunshine, Layla's demeanor turned a bit more sheepish. "Not to be crass, gentlemen, but shirts off, hats on."

There were good-natured chuckles as the men followed instructions. Jace bent his elbow behind his head and grabbed the back of his collar, tugging off the T-shirt. When he'd shrugged free of the material, his eyes met Layla's and her cheeks flushed a rosy pink. She quickly glanced away, erasing his earlier pangs of jealousy. Quincy could flirt and joke all he wanted. The sight of *his* chest didn't make Layla blush.

Jace balled up his shirt and was prepared to toss it

on the ground, but Jarrett walked past him to hang his long-sleeved shirt from a fence post.

Layla snapped her fingers. "I have a great idea for a cover! Can I borrow someone's hat?"

Jace and Quincy both stepped forward at the same time, but Jace quickly moved in front of the other man. "Here."

"Thanks." Layla smiled up at him, but shyly avoided his gaze, and he was reminded of moments like these when they were teenagers. How had he not realized sooner that she was attracted to him? Or maybe he'd known on some level but had been content to stay in denial because she was his best friend's little sister. There was an unwritten code among guys. Chris and Jace had candidly discussed wanting to make out with girls they thought were hot, but Chris would have kicked his ass if he'd ever talked about Layla that way.

Layla took some of the discarded shirts and hung them over the wooden slats, leaving Jace's cowboy hat over the post at the end. She took several shots from different angles, and watching her work was sexy in its own right. Jace knew from the pictures on her gallery website that she was good at what she did. But it was captivating to watch her intense focus, the energy in her posture, the way she momentarily forgot that any of them—even him—were there.

She was smiling when she straightened, and Jace's urge to kiss her this time had nothing to do with possessiveness. "Perfect. Pretty day, picturesque paddock and a couple of masculine clothing articles to hint at the contents inside. That gives us a family-friendly front cover no one could object to at the local store."

"Much appreciated," Grayson said. "I could just tell

anyone who complained to get over it, but I'd prefer to avoid alienating customers."

Layla nodded. "I'm sure the sponsors listed on the back would like to keep paying customers happy, too."

A breeze kicked up, and Quincy shivered comically. "Can we move this along before the talent freezes to death?"

Jace was immune to the wind. Just looking in Layla's direction kept him plenty warm.

"Okay, let's figure out how to arrange you. This isn't a bad class photo—you shouldn't all just be standing in a line according to height. We want some depth of composition." She came over to them, considering, and asked Jarrett to stand on the other side of the fence, leaning against it. "Like this," Layla demonstrated, folding her arms atop the wood. "Great forearm display. Trust me, women go for that."

"We really do," Sierra called, strolling up the path with Hadley.

Layla turned, surprise evident on her face. "Weren't you going to the movies?"

Hadley shrugged. "Becca called and told us it was sold out. So we came back to see if we could—"

"Ogle."

"—help."

Layla laughed. "Maybe it will be helpful for me to get someone else's opinion on how things look."

"But you're only allowed to ogle me," Jarrett called to his wife with a mock glare.

She blew him a kiss. "No problem. I'd happily stare at you all day."

Quincy cleared his throat. "Uh, you guys mind leaving the rest of us out of your foreplay?"

Laughter rippled through the group, and Layla returned to arranging the men where she wanted them. As she had with Jarrett, she would demonstrate the exact pose she was looking for, then she would make hands-on adjustments, fine-tuning body language, the tilt of the head, even the smallest angle of a hat brim, occasionally glancing to Sierra and Hadley for nods of approval. When she got to Jace, however, she stiffened briefly, as if hesitant to touch him. It would have felt like rejection, except that the flare of heat in her gaze before she lowered her lashes gave her away.

He couldn't resist fanning the flame. "How do you want me?" he asked, the words casual even if the erotic images in his mind were anything but.

She was close enough that he could see the rise and fall of her chest as her breathing quickened. "I, ah..." She leaned back, jerking her chin toward Hugh. "Just stand like him but with the opposite arm at your side. You two will mirror each other and bookend the group."

With that, she retreated behind the lens, testing the light before she began taking pictures in earnest. Jace grinned. She was nowhere near immune to him. While there might not be much he could do about it in the group setting, it would be time for his solo portrait soon enough. *Can't avoid me forever, beautiful.*

"Layla, hold up!"

With her hand on the car door, Layla paused and turned back to see Sierra emerge from the ranch house, a foil-wrapped container in her hands.

"It seemed wrong to let the person who did all the work leave without something to eat," Sierra said. Earlier, Sierra had gone into the house and ordered pizza to be delivered so that when the photo session was done, there'd be something to feed the guys. Layla had appreciated the forethought. "I ordered way too much, especially since Grayson and Hadley left to pick up the twins. If you're not going to stay, at least take some with you."

"Thank you," Layla said. She'd declined the offer of staying to eat with the others, stating that she should get back to her daughter. Jace's expression had turned to one of yearning, so fierce that she'd expected everyone in the room to remark on it, to realize that Addie was his daughter, too.

"I put in enough for your little girl, too," Sierra added.

"Theoretically, she's just finishing up dinner with her grandpa, but now she has pizza to snack on later. You'll be her favorite person." *As long as you don't insult the opening sequences in* The Wizard of Oz. "I really appreciate your input today—and your being all right with Jarrett posing in the calendar."

"I know how devastated he was after his sister's car accident a few years ago. She's fine now, but he felt so helpless. It's fantastic that you came up with something tangible you can do for Chris and his family. Jarrett is honored to be a part of it, and there's no way I ever could have objected to that." She stood there a moment, not yet handing over the pizza.

"Was there something else?" Layla asked.

"Well, we haven't known each other very long, so I might be overstepping with what I'm about to say." She smiled mischievously. "Luckily, I am okay with that. Watching you today, I couldn't help but notice that you had a pretty strong reaction to Jace."

"Wh-what?" Damn. She hadn't realized she'd been so transparent. Had the other men noticed, or had it been more obvious to someone observing from a distance? "I don't know what you mean."

Sierra arched an eyebrow. "Boy, are you a terrible liar."

Layla's face heated, and she relented with a half truth. "I had a crush on him when we were teenagers. There may be lingering nostalgia, but it doesn't mean anything."

"Do you want it to mean something? Because I've gotten to know the Trent brothers through Jarrett, and I've never seen Jace look at anyone the way he was watching you."

A rush of joy went through Layla. "Really?"

"Maybe we could double-date sometime."

The joy ebbed. "Well, I'm—"

"Once you're done with the calendar and not as busy," Sierra added.

"Thanks for the offer—you seem like a lot of fun to hang out with—but once the calendar is done, I'll be leaving." One of the many reasons it wouldn't do to dwell on how Jace Trent might or might not be looking for her. "I won't be in Cupid's Bow long."

"I said that exact same thing a few years ago." Laughing, Sierra held up her left hand. The sun glinted off her golden wedding band. "And now I live here with the love of my life."

"Should it make me nervous that our womenfolk are bonding?" Jarrett asked, staring out the kitchen window.

"Hmmm?" Jace barely heard him. As he leaned against the counter finishing his slice of pizza, he was mentally replaying his favorite moments of the day. He wished his one-on-one photo session with Layla was sooner. She'd scheduled Hugh for tomorrow and Grayson for the day after, but Jace wasn't until next week. He wanted to tell himself that she was saving the best for last, but he knew what she was doing—avoiding him and their mutual attraction. "Wait, did you just say *our womenfolk*?"

"Sierra and Layla. They're both sharp ladies. If they ever conspired against us, we'd be toast."

"Layla isn't 'my' anything."

Jarrett rolled his eyes. "Don't you ever get tired of being the perpetual bachelor? Quit being afraid of finding something real."

"You're a dumbass," Jace said mildly. "I'm not afraid." *She is.*

"So you admit you like her?"

"Whole-heartedly."

Their conversation had drawn the attention of the Washington brothers. Quincy glanced up from the kitchen table with a groan. "Dammit. Does this mean I can't ask her out?"

Jace nodded adamantly.

"Well, hold on, now," Hugh told Jace. "You can't knock Quincy out of the running unless you're prepared to ask her out yourself. Does she know you like her?"

He was pretty sure he'd made that clear last time he'd kissed her. "I think so, but it's complicated." Although he couldn't tell them the whole story, he could at least vent some of his frustration. "She's a single mom, and I didn't make a great first impression on her daughter. Pretty sure the kid hates me." It hurt his heart to admit that out loud. Layla had assured him that Addie would come around eventually, but what if she didn't? "I tried to befriend her. I brought her a stuffed horse and—"

Quincy laughed. "What is it with every little girl wanting a pony?"

"Actually," Jace said, "I don't think she even likes horses."

"Do you know how I proposed to Sierra?" Jarrett asked.

"Dude, I thought we were talking about my life."

Hugh rolled his eyes in Jarrett's direction. "You know how it is with this one—all roads lead back to the red-head."

Jarrett ignored them. "I wrote out my proposal on a napkin and left it with her morning coffee."

"And she said yes to that?" Quincy said incredulously.

"Long story, but it had meaning for us. You don't necessarily win someone over because you assume every little girl wants a pony. Hell, Trent, you should know that. How different are Alyssa and Mandy? What makes a perfect gift for one of your nieces might not interest the other one at all."

"True." He was eager to try again with Addie, but Layla hadn't suggested another meeting.

Hell, she'd barely stuck around long enough for him to even ask about it. *Are you going to let that stop you?* No. Definitely not. If she wasn't going to give him an opportunity, he'd just have to create his own.

Chapter 10

Although it was a relief to see her brother out of the hospital bed, free of IV tubes and monitor wires, Layla's heart still twisted at the strain etched into his usually smiling face. With help from friends and family, Suzanne had turned the living room into recovery headquarters. Chris was stationed on the couch, with a remote control, his phone, bottled water and assorted medications all within easy reach. When Layla had arrived twenty minutes ago, he'd joked about the perfect existence—"a beautiful wife and all the binge-watching a man could want"—but he was clearly frustrated by his lack of mobility. He kept staring through the window into the backyard where Addie and Suzanne were blowing bubbles. The twins were napping now, but whenever one of his daughters cried, his jaw tightened, and Layla knew he hated that he wasn't more help with the babies.

"It's temporary," she offered.

He turned back toward her, his expression puzzled. "What were we talking about?"

Nothing really—because he'd trailed off midsentence a few minutes ago, and she'd been trying to decide what to say. She could hardly tell him how she'd spent her day so far, since it had involved taking pictures of Hugh Washington for Project Secret Calendar. "You just had a look on your face like you desperately want to get off the couch, so I was reminding you that before too long, you'll be on your feet again. Sierra will see to that."

Layla thought about her new friend's comments yesterday. *I've never seen Jace look at anyone the way he was watching you.* It was unwise to let the observation make her giddy, yet every time she thought of Sierra's words, she felt a tingle down to her toes.

"What are you grinning about?" Chris asked suspiciously.

Oops. "Was I? I'm…just really glad you're out of the hospital."

He grimaced. "I was, too, at first. But at least in the hospital, there were nurses and staff. I feel awful that Suzanne has to take care of me by herself when she already has her hands full with the twins."

Layla bit her lip. Did he wonder why *she* wasn't spending more time here at the house? Maybe she should tell him about the calendar so he understood that she was trying to help even when she wasn't present. "Maybe I could make my visits longer. Addie's kindergarten teacher has been emailing me worksheets, so those might help keep her occu—"

"Not necessary. I was feeling sorry for myself, not trying to inconvenience anyone further. Honestly, I should be counting my blessings that we have so much help. Mom offered to spend the nights here to be on hand for her granddaughters. We haven't felt desperate enough to take her up on it yet, but it's nice to know the offer's there." He raised an eyebrow. "Speaking of Mom, neither of you has said much about the other one. I was expecting hysterics or outraged monologues...or, at the very least, minor griping. Have y'all reached a truce?"

"Something like that." Truthfully, the time Layla was spending on calendar plans gave her an acceptable reason to avoid her mother. She hadn't told Claire the specifics, but she'd confided that she was working on a surprise to help Chris and Suzanne. Given how much Claire adored her son, that had been sufficient to excuse Layla from some of their otherwise awkward mother-daughter time. Hopefully, Claire's approval would last once she discovered the project revolved around her daughter spending a lot of time with half-clothed men. Layla had endured more than enough pearl-clutching, what-will-people-think lectures.

Of course, Claire's response to the calendar couldn't be nearly as scathing as her reaction to learning Martin was in town. Layla sighed. Her father had asked her— if she found an opportunity where it felt right—to talk to Chris on his behalf. She wasn't eager to broach the subject, hating when it felt like she and Chris had to take sides on their parents' problems, but she supposed this was the best opportunity she was likely to have.

"Hey, can I talk to you about something?" she asked.

"Of course. I mean, unless it's some lady medical problem. In which case, I beg you, go talk to my wife instead."

Layla chuckled, the sound rusty with nerves. "Nothing like that. It's…about our family. When was the last time you talked to Dad?"

His expression grew stony. "Not much to say to him after the hell he put Mom through."

Layla took a deep breath. She knew from past experience how protective Chris was of their mother, and she didn't want to get sucked into an argument about their parents. "Granted, he was a terrible husband."

"And a selfish SOB of a father," Chris interrupted. "We live in a small town, and he didn't care at all that his actions affected us. Do you know I got into a fistfight my sophomore year because Bobby Grendale blamed Dad—and somehow, by extension, our whole family— for breaking up his parents' marriage by sleeping with his mom?"

She winced. "I vaguely remember that."

"When Dad left Cupid's Bow, he didn't just leave Mom. He abandoned us, you and me. I'll never understand how you could choose to go live with him. It *wrecked* her."

"Okay, but that was years ago. This might be hard for you to fathom, but Dad has really been there for me. He's changed. He's not self-absorbed, and he's not a womanizer. He dotes on Addie, he misses you and… he's here in town."

"What?" Red blotches mottled Chris's face. "Since when?"

"Not long," she evaded. Chris didn't need all the details of Martin's reunion with Gena the other night. Frankly, it was pure luck that Addie hadn't mentioned it already. "He's worried about you. He wants to see you."

"Mom would hate that."

Layla tamped down the familiar annoyance. "You and

I are both parents ourselves now. Wouldn't you always want what's best for your girls? Seeing Dad could be cathartic for you. Mom has to understand that, deep down. She shouldn't make it about her." *Like she did when she found out about my pregnancy.* "Please, Chris. I know you and Mom are close, but you can't make life decisions based on whether or not she might get her feelings hurt."

He glared.

Sensing protest, she cut him off before he had a chance to say anything. "Don't you think people should be forgiven for past mistakes?" *Please say yes.* One day very soon, she was going to have another difficult conversation with Chris, and she couldn't bear the thought that he might hate her or Jace.

"Depends on the person," he grated. "Depends on the mistake."

Not the most reassuring thing he could've said, but it was better than a flat no. "Will you at least promise to think about it?"

After he grudgingly agreed, she said she should probably collect Addie and head back to Gena's. Her cousin would be home from the bank in an hour or so, and Layla wanted time to figure out a dinner plan. She was trying to pitch in as much as possible to show her gratitude for everything Gena had done.

On the drive, Addie was uncharacteristically animated. She talked about how cute the twin babies were and how much fun she'd had playing with Aunt Suzanne. Her daughter's enthusiasm caused a twinge in Layla's chest. Layla couldn't begin to imagine moving back, but would visits really have been that difficult? Addie might have benefitted from more frequent interaction with loving family members.

She stole a glance at her daughter in the rearview mirror. Despite Layla's pensive mood, she couldn't help grinning at the adult-sized straw cowboy hat sliding down over Addie's eyes. Suzanne had run across it earlier while looking for the bubble wands and insisted Addie take it since *every Texas girl needs her own hat*. Addie had scoffed that a tornado would easily dislodge a hat, and Suzanne had convinced her niece to look at a hat as a kind of early warning system—"If the wind gets strong enough to blow your hat away, maybe it's a sign that you should go inside."

After that bit of logic, Addie hadn't taken the hat off once. Layla had images of her daughter wearing it to bed or in the bathtub. Claire's rule had always been no hats at the dinner table, but Layla was willing to make exceptions.

"What should I cook tonight? And don't say pizza," Layla preempted. "You've had it twice recently. We should come up with something else."

Addie giggled. "But I like pizza."

"Well, sure, but—" Layla's eyes widened at the sight of the truck parked in front of Gena's house. Jace! Her pulse fluttered, and she couldn't tell if the reaction was joy, anxiety or both.

Part of her was genuinely pleased by his presence, but Addie didn't take surprises well. After a rocky first impression, was he about to make a worst second impression on his daughter? Was it too late to throw the car in Reverse and pretend she'd never been here? Layla mentally kicked herself. *I should've just suggested Gena meet us in town for barbecue.*

"Oh, look." She tried to make her voice bright. "Mr. Jace is paying us a visit."

Addie's face scrunched into a scowl. "What's he doing here?"

That's what I'd like to know. "I'm not sure. Let's go say hi and find out." Without giving her daughter time to argue—or herself time to second-guess the decision—Layla reached for the handle of her car door. In lieu of a chance to check her hair or apply a fresh coat of lip gloss, she smoothed a hand over the skirt of her cotton sundress and hoped for the best.

Addie trudged along beside her, making it clear with a series of heavy sighs that she was doing so under duress.

Jace was sitting on the front porch, but he stood as they approached. He beamed at them with his usual confidence, no trace of the self-doubt he'd expressed last time he was here. "Hello, Dempsey ladies!"

Addie tipped back her hat to glare at him, and Layla almost laughed at a whimsical mental image of her daughter challenging him to a quick draw. "Hi. Mama, can I go inside now?"

"Not so fast, partner." Jace tapped the brim of the straw hat. "Don't you want to see the present I got you?"

This prompted another dramatic sigh, and Layla intervened before her daughter commented on his gift-giving abilities. "Manners, Addison Rose."

"Okay." It was unclear which adult Addie was answering, but Jace smiled, clearly encouraged.

He held out a dark green gift bag. "Be careful opening it. It's breakable."

Layla rolled her eyes inwardly. Did he really have to get the six-year-old something fragile? But Addie dutifully sat down, removing the tissue paper with care. Finally, she extracted some kind of jar with water in it, mounted on a cylindrical base.

"I don't know what this is," she said. It wasn't a complaint, just a statement. She sounded intrigued.

Jace sat next to her. "See this button on the bottom? Push that."

Addie did as instructed, and a faint blue light shone up through the water, accompanied by a soft whirring. Then the water began to move in a circle, and moments later, there was a funnel of water spinning that perfectly mimicked the shape and motion of a tornado. Addie's mouth fell open, her gaze awestruck.

"Mama! Look!"

"I see." But Layla wasn't watching the obviously homemade tornado machine. She couldn't keep her eyes off Jace. He'd never looked more attractive, the sunlight highlighting the happiness in his blue eyes as he grinned at their daughter. "You made this?"

He nodded.

Addie stared at him with something like hero worship. "You *did*? Can you teach me how?"

"Not tonight—we'd need to buy parts—but someday I will. Promise."

Layla almost flinched at that. It wasn't a good idea to make casual promises to children, especially one who could be as literal-minded and dogged as hers, but right now, she was too moved by Jace's thoughtfulness to dwell on potential mistakes.

Addison's eyes fell on the cooler a few feet away. "What's in there? Is that for me, too?"

He laughed. "Technically, yes, but I'm not sure you'll find the contents very exciting. I brought food. I was hoping to cook for you and your mom. And your aunt Gena, of course, when she gets home."

Layla blinked. It was difficult to resist a good-looking

man who made your daughter presents and offered to cook for you. "You want to cook for us?"

"Do you know how to make pizza?" Addie asked.

"Never tried," he said. "Maybe another time. For now, I thought I'd throw some burgers on the grill and cook some French fries. I also brought ice cream with me. Ever tried fries dipped in milk shakes?"

"I love them!" Addie glowed up at him in pure six-year-old bliss. "How did you know?"

He winked over the top of her head at Layla. "I had a hunch. So, what do you ladies say? Can I stay for dinner?"

It would take a heart of stone to refuse, and Layla's heart was currently melted into a gooey puddle. "Of course."

Addie tugged her mom's skirt. "Can I change clothes? I want to look special."

"Sure, honey." Too bad they'd left Addie's dress-up ruby slippers back at home. "I think Mr. Jace would like that." Layla had barely unlocked the front door before her daughter dashed past, with both Layla and Jace calling after her to remind her to be careful with the tornado machine.

Layla turned to the surprising man at her side. "I can't believe you made that for her."

"It was nothing." He ducked his gaze, rubbing the back of his neck. "Just needed some online how-to videos, patience, trial and error...plus a few common household supplies."

"Common?"

"Sure. Empty salsa jar, a glue gun, rubber bands, a motor, LED lights, high-density polyethylene. You know, the kind of stuff most moms probably carry around in their purses."

She laughed. "How long did it take?"

"What gets me more points with you—saying it took no time at all, which makes me sound like a technologically gifted badass, or saying that I worked all last night into the wee hours of the morning, which makes me sound dedicated and thorough?"

"I'm sure a little of both is true." Impulsively, she leaned forward and kissed his cheek.

He reached up to snag her around the waist. "It would have been worth staying up all night for that." His voice was low, no longer playful. He sounded completely sincere.

She blushed. "Don't read too much into it. It was just a platonic peck between friends."

His gaze locked with hers. She didn't know what he was thinking exactly, but she knew what this proximity was doing to her. Heat swirled low in her belly, and her mouth was suddenly dry. *Kiss him for real.* Lord knew she wanted to, but that would make her a total hypocrite. She'd been the one to insist they not complicate matters with physical interaction, and she stood by that decision. Kind of.

Trying not to stare at his mouth, she took a half step back. "Why don't you go grab the cooler? We should get the ice cream in the freezer and the fries in the oven." Or she could just press the bag of frozen potatoes against her flushed face and cook them that way. A few minutes alone with Jace was enough to heat the entire kitchen. Would it always be like this? Years ago, her body had burned for his, even though she'd been too young to know what she was doing. Now she had more knowledge and experience, and she couldn't help fantasizing about how being with him could be even better.

"How do I look, Mama?"

Layla turned to see her daughter wobbling in the doorway; with effort, Layla smothered a chuckle that might hurt Addie's feelings. "Aren't those Aunt Gena's boots?" The black cowgirl boots with turquoise embellishments came almost to Addie's knees.

"Cowgirl boots to go with the cowgirl hat." Sure enough, Addie was still wearing the straw hat—along with a red sequined dress that Layla had bought her last Christmas. She held her arms out proudly. "I found the dress inside the underneath of my suitcase."

Inside the underneath? *The lining.* There was a rip in the suitcase's lining. The dress must have slipped down inside it without Layla's noticing.

"Are you sure that's what you want to wear?" Layla asked gently. "You won't be upset if you spill ketchup or mustard or ice cream on your dress?"

"I'll be extra careful," Addie promised.

"All right, then the hat and dress stay. But you should probably lose the boots since you didn't ask Aunt Gena's permission."

"I don't know," Jace drawled from behind Layla. "The boots make the outfit. You look smashing, Addie! You could have a real future as a fashion designer."

She gave him a withering look. "I'm gonna be a meteorologist."

He chuckled as she stomped around the corner to return the boots to Gena's closet. "Well. She told me. Guess I'd better get to work on dinner and see if I can win her back."

Once he was out of the kitchen, it was easier to

breathe. Layla's heart rate slowed back to normal, and her skin didn't tingle quite so much—although she did steal the occasional peek out the window to watch him at the grill.

"Um, cuz?" Gena asked when she came home. "Want to fill me in on why there's a sexy Trent brother cooking in my yard? Not that I'm complaining, mind you. I'm just a little surprised after his last visit to see him again so—"

"Aunt Gena! Come see what Mr. Jace gave me," Addie demanded happily.

Gena raised an eyebrow, whispering to Layla, "He resorted to bribery?"

"Tornado bribery."

"Well played. This guy is good."

And so were his hamburgers. Half an hour later, the four of them sat around the table, happily devouring burgers, fries and chocolate milk shakes.

Layla dunked a fry into her shake, groaning in a combination of pleasure and guilt. "A better mother would have made sure there were more vegetables on this table."

"Pffft." Jace waved a hand. "The burgers have lettuce, tomato, onions and pickles."

"Which are really just cucumbers," Gena chimed in.

Jace nodded. "So it's practically a salad."

Addie giggled, knocking her cowgirl hat askew, and Layla's heart soared at the genuine happiness on her daughter's face. Tonight had been such a wonderful surprise, and Addie obviously didn't want it to end yet. "After dinner, wanna watch *The Wizard of Oz* with me?" she invited Jace.

"Even better," he said, "I brought over a new movie

to show you. It's called *Twister*. It has a bunch of torna-does in it, way more than *The Wizard of Oz*."

Addie's eyes widened. "Really?"

"Uh…" There were reasons Layla had never shown her daughter one of the most famous tornado movies. "Addie and I have already had a pretty exciting day. Maybe we should stick with *The Wizard of Oz* for to-night and save *Twister* for another time." Like, two or three years from now. The CGI special effects were a bit scarier than a black-and-white cyclone from the 1930s.

"Aw." Addie stuck her bottom lip out.

"Or," Layla countered, "you could just go to bed after dinner."

The pout quickly disappeared.

Layla affectionately straightened her daughter's hat. "That's what I thought."

After dinner, Gena made a big show of yawning and stretching and saying she'd had a long day at work. "Think I'll turn in early," she said.

"Can we have popcorn?" Addie asked Layla.

"Of course," Jace answered. "What's a movie with-out popcorn?"

Layla smacked her palm to her forehead. "On top of fries and ice cream? Definitely not."

Jace smirked. "You forget, I once saw *you* eat three funnel cakes, a box of caramel corn and a strawberry sundae in one afternoon at the Harvest Day Festival."

"All of which I threw up after the Tilt-A-Whirl," she recalled with a grimace.

Addie's eyes were wide. "What's a Tilt-A-Whirl?"

"An instrument of torture your uncle Chris and Mr. Jace dared me to ride."

Jace laughed. "Oh, please. We never had to dare you

to do anything. You had the guts to join our adventures voluntarily."

Because you were there. Maybe there'd been a time during her elementary years when she'd wanted to be like her big brother, but by the time she was a teenager, Chris was no longer the motivating factor. She'd loved being around Jace. Tonight had been a strong reminder why. He was funny and charming and, despite occasional teasing obnoxiousness, thoughtful.

He caught her studying him and raised an eyebrow in silent question.

She deflected by turning to her daughter. "Okay, fine, we can share a bowl of popcorn. But only if you hurry and put on pajamas while I make it."

As soon as her daughter was out of earshot, Layla turned to Jace. "Thank you for tonight. She's having a blast. But I wish you'd run it past me before offering to let her watch *Twister*. Characters actually die in that movie! That's way more intense than *The Wizard of Oz*."

"You're obviously forgetting about Dorothy's homicidal tendencies toward wicked witches."

She bit the inside of her lip, refusing to laugh. "A couple of nights ago, she kept me awake kicking after she crawled into bed after nightmares. I don't even want to think about the bad dreams the special effects in *Twister* could give her." She cocked her head, trying to remember the last time she'd watched the movie. "Plus, isn't one of the characters a sex therapist?"

"Um…maybe? I didn't think it would be a big deal. Cole's daughter Mandy loves *Twister*, and she's not that much older than Addie."

Was Layla overreacting? Now that she thought about it, there was a four-year-old boy who lived on their street who claimed *Jurassic Park* as his favorite movie. "Honestly, I'm not sure how big a deal it would be. It's been so long since I've seen it that I'm not one-hundred-percent sure how she'd react. But be careful what you say to her or offer her without running it by me first." She sighed. "Do I sound like a horrible control freak?"

He gave her a boyishly lopsided smile. "You sound like a concerned mom."

"Thanks for understanding."

"I may be new at all of this, but I'm trying."

He really was. She was moved by how good he'd been with Addie for the past hour. He could be silly with her, but he also took her seriously. When Addie talked to him, he didn't look at his phone or absently nod like an adult whose attention had wandered. He leaned forward with alert interest, making it clear with his posture and body language that he considered her important.

The freshly popped popcorn smelled so good that Layla was glad she'd let them talk her into it. She carried the bowl and napkins while Addie raced ahead to turn on the DVD player. However, once they were all seated on the couch, with Addie snuggled between them, the little girl showed no urgency for starting the movie. Instead, she asked Jace if there were other things besides the festival he'd done with Chris and Layla.

"Oh, sure. Your uncle and your mama were two of my best friends. We went to movies together, rode bikes together, went fishing… Your mom is *terrible* at fishing," he confided in a stage whisper.

"I am not!" Layla objected.

"You used to scare the fish away with all your loud giggling."

"That was one time—and only because *you* were tickling me."

"True." Jace held up his hands and wiggled his fingers at Addie. "What about you, kiddo? Are you ticklish?"

Addie shrieked with delight and tried to hide behind her mom. The battle escalated to Jace trying to tickle each of them with one hand while Layla and Addie retaliated with throw pillows. Unfortunately, the battle had casualties—the bowl of popcorn landed upside down in the floor.

"Oops." Layla stood. "I'd better get the dustpan. And we'd better settle down and behave. Addie, do you want to help me make more popcorn?"

But Addie was looking solemnly at Jace. "Do you know Uncle Chris got hurt?"

He nodded. "I visited him every day in the hospital to help keep him company until you and your mom got here."

"He's not in the hospital anymore," Addie said. "We went to his house today. But he's still hurt."

"I know, but he's getting better," Jace reassured her. "Even though he's out of the hospital, he has good doctors still helping him. And other people, too. Like your mom. Do you know she came up with a way to help him by taking pictures? She's a smart lady."

"She's making a calendar," Addie said. "That's why I visited the bank this morning with Gena, so Mommy could take pictures. Gena told another bank lady that there were hot men with no shirts, but I think she meant cold men. People with no shirts would be cold."

Layla choked on a laugh as Jace flushed red. *I should remind Gena that kids overhear more than people think.*

"So," she interrupted, "how about we get that movie started?"

She excused herself during the opening credits to get a glass of water. When she returned, her heart did a slow, sweet somersault at the sight of Addie tucked against Jace's chest, her sleepy eyes at half-mast. By the time Dorothy met the traveling "fortune teller," Addie was snoring loudly enough to drown out the musical score.

"Here." Layla reached for her daughter. "You're probably losing feeling in your arm. I'll take her to bed."

Jace met her gaze over Addie's head. "Let me. Please." Was it a trick of the flickering light from the TV, or were his eyes damp?

Layla nodded, struck momentarily wordless by a lump of emotion in her throat. As Jace rose, cradling Addie close to him, Layla hit the mute button on the remote. But she left the TV on to help illuminate the path. She led him down the hallway of the still, silent house to Addie's room. While Jace tucked their daughter into the blankets, Layla turned on the projector nightlight on the other side of the bed. Dimly lit stars began spinning on the ceiling above Addie. Suddenly, Layla wished she could just telepathically share with Jace the million little things he'd missed—about the day Addie picked out the star lamp during a trip to the museum and how she'd later lost her first baby tooth on the ride home. About how the hand-knit blanket Jace had just pulled over her had been a gift from Layla's first regular client. About the day Addie met Meredith and made her first real friend.

If Layla had found the courage to tell Jace she was pregnant seven years ago, would he have been there for all those moments? Would this be their life together;

tickle fights after dinner and tucking their daughter into bed? Because of Layla's choices, they'd never know what could have been. Eyes stinging, she pressed a kiss to Addie's forehead and retreated from the room.

Jace followed closely. As always, her body hummed at his nearness.

"I don't have to go yet," he said, his voice barely a whisper. "We could watch *Twister*. It would be like a refresher course for you."

Her eyes strayed to the sofa a few feet away as she imagined spending the next couple of hours there with him. "I can't." But it was so tempting. She'd like nothing more than to snuggle against him with the same carefree affection her daughter had shown.

His expression was knowing. "I understand."

She was afraid he did. If things were different… "I want to go over the shots I took today, do some editing, get a feel for what's working before I meet Grayson tomorrow. I think this calendar might actually turn out really well."

"Never doubted it."

His matter-of-fact belief in her warmed her from the inside like a sip of rich hot cocoa. "Thank you again for tonight. It meant a lot to her."

His smile was bittersweet. "Not nearly as much as it did to me, beautiful. This is what I want, more of this. Hearing what she wants to be when she grows up, chatting with her over dinner, getting to tuck her in at night. I don't want to be *Mr. Jace*. I want to be Daddy."

Would he still feel that way once the novelty had worn off? Or what about when he started dating someone new and having a child was inconvenient? Layla was starting to believe he was capable of the long-term commitment. She just wasn't sure yet how it would work from two different cities with their very different lives. And she had no idea how her daughter would take it.

"We'll figure out a way to tell her, a way to make all this work," Layla said. "It just takes time."

"I've already lost six years."

She winced.

"Layla, I'm sorry. I wasn't trying to—"

"I know." She squeezed his hand, but quickly dropped it. "You were only telling the truth."

"How soon can I see her again?"

"I'll call you. I'm not sure yet how the next couple of days will play out. I told Chris that Dad was in town, and he promised to think about seeing him. If Chris goes through with it, they may need me there to keep the peace."

"You worried Chris will try to beat up your father with his crutches?"

"I know you're teasing, but the thought *has* crossed my mind."

"And telling Chris about us?" he pressed. "When can we do that? Now that I know Addie's mine, I feel like I'll blurt out the truth whenever I'm in the room with him. I don't know how you kept the secret so long."

"I don't know how, either." There were times when the heaviness of the truth weighed on her like a physical burden. As nervous as she was about the truth getting out, it would also be a relief.

"We have a lot to sort through," she said. "But another time? I really do have work to do on this calendar." At least that way, if Chris ruptured stitches taking a swing at Jace, Suzanne would have a head start on his medical bills.

* * *

"Can't sleep?" Gena's expression was obscured in the dim lighting that came from above the kitchen sink, but the sympathy in her voice was evident.

"Not sure," Layla said from the table. "I haven't actually tried yet." It was two in the morning. She'd long since finished her photo proofs, yet here she still sat.

Gena shuffled to the fridge to fill a glass with water. "Stressed?"

"Yes and no." Layla idly stirred a spoon in the mug of peppermint tea that had grown cold. "I am stressed about all kinds of family things—whether it's too late for Dad and Chris to repair their relationship, how to tell Addie the truth about things, Chris's recovery… But, honestly, it's not stress that's keeping me up. It's almost the opposite. I had such a good time tonight."

"And staying awake is your way of not letting the night end yet."

"Something like that." She'd been reliving each moment, frame by frame, right up until the moment when Jace had kissed her goodbye on the cheek. It had been a brief, innocent touch—and yet she'd had to splash cold water on her face as his truck pulled out of the driveway.

"I heard you puttering around the kitchen a while ago," Gena said. She nodded toward the mug on the table. "Making tea, I guess. At first, I hoped the noise was you and Jace making out in the kitchen."

"Of course not! I told you—we agreed that it was more sensible to keep our relationship platonic."

Gena rolled her eyes. "'Sensible' does not equal fun. You used to have all sorts of fun, remember?"

"I also remember I got grounded a lot."

"My point is, don't let being a mom and a grown-up

rob you of the best parts of yourself. Addie is a great kid. I love her. But she's pretty serious for a kindergartner. Tonight, laughing with Jace, she embraced her fun side. You want that for her, right? Then you have to set the example. Don't be afraid to enjoy your life, to go after what you want."

"Enabler." Where had this advice been hours ago when Layla had been talking herself out of cuddling into Jace's side for a nice long tornado movie?

"Friend," Gena corrected. "You know I only want what's best for you."

And that included making out with Jace Trent? Debatable. On the other hand...

"I've thought a lot tonight about regret," Layla admitted. "Jace helped me get Addie into bed, and watching them together, thinking about what kind of father he could have been—"

"Still can be."

"It's been seven years since I chickened out of telling him I was pregnant. I'm starting to regret that I didn't. I'm not sure getting into a romantic or physical relationship with him is wise, but..."

"You don't want to look back later and regret not trying?"

"Do I sound like a wishy-washy person who doesn't know what she wants?"

"Yes." When Layla spluttered in outrage, Gena laughed. "But that's most of the human race. We're never one-hundred-percent sure what direction our lives should go. Even when we know what we want, sometimes we can't immediately define how to get it. Or we get it, and it turns out to be far different than we expected. You never know unless you try."

And if she tried and failed?

Would that be better or worse than returning home without kissing Jace again, without finding out what might exist between them?

As Gena said, there was only one way to find out.

Jace had never understood the term *quit while you're ahead.* He'd quit plenty of things in his life, including college, but only because he knew in his gut that a situation wasn't going to work out. *That's* when you cut your losses and bailed, not when something was actually working. When you were ahead, you graciously accepted the encouragement from the universe and pressed your advantage. So, after last night's success at Gena's, here he was, sitting on the tailgate of his truck, hoping to duplicate—or even improve—his results.

Assuming Layla didn't kick his ass for hijacking her photo shoot.

Technically, she was supposed to be meeting Jace's business partner today at the Whippoorwill farm. Thanks to Jace's intervention, however, she'd get to take some pictures for the calendar *and* they would get to continue their conversation from last night. They needed to talk more with no chance of Addie waking up and hearing them. *Admit it, talking isn't all you want to do.* True. He wanted Layla, and he refused to feel guilty about it. Based on her pretty blushes and the dewy-eyed glances that lasted a few seconds too long and the way her breathing quickened when he was close, he wasn't alone in his desires.

Whether she decided to act on those desires or not, he considered the time alone with her today worthwhile. Worst-case scenario, she'd be annoyed that he'd changed the modeling schedule without asking her. Even if that happened, he'd get to spend a little time sitting in the shade of the barn on a lovely autumn day, and he'd get to see the woman who'd been haunting more and more of his thoughts for the past week. *And here she comes.*

She drove down the well-worn dirt path that led to the barn. He couldn't tell from the other side of the windshield when she realized it was him. She was shaking her head as she climbed out of the car seconds later.

An oversize pair of tortoiseshell sunglasses hid her eyes, but her lips twitched in the suggestion of amusement, despite the exasperation in her voice. "You have *got* to be kidding me."

He gave her a small wave and his most winning smile. "Grayson had to cancel." After an hour of cajoling on Jace's part and input from Hadley, a die-hard romantic. "So I heroically offered to step in."

"Uh-huh." Layla wagged an accusing finger at him as she marched forward, her legs long and tanned beneath the hem of her denim shorts. "You said I had a bad habit of running away. Know what your bad habit is, Trent?"

"I have so many. Can you be more specific?"

She socked him gently in the shoulder. "Ambushing people. This makes twice in two days."

Guilty as charged. "Well…yeah. When I ambush you, it gives you less of a chance to run away."

She shoved the sunglasses on top of her head, her eyes meeting his. There was a wicked glint in her gaze, and, for a second, he wondered if she planned to sock him again. Or worse. Instead, she bent forward. Her breath feathered against his cheek. "I'm not running away now, am I?"

Jace's pulse pounded in his ears as she clasped her

fingers behind his neck. He slid down from the back of the truck, standing so that he could pull her body against his. A man could easily get addicted to the lush feel of her curves. "Layla." The whispered word was a declaration of praise and a plea for permission all wrapped in one.

Her hazel eyes stayed open until the last second, dark graceful lashes sweeping down as his mouth took hers. Damn, he was starving for her. He deepened the kiss, dropping his hands to her hips.

Wishing he could kiss her everywhere at once, he trailed his lips over the soft skin of her throat, nipping at her here and there, wondering if she'd stop him if he kept going lower. He hesitated, waiting to see if she voiced any objection, before undoing just the top button of her shirt. The sight of lace-covered cleavage left him dizzy and aching. He palmed one breast, and her soft moan of encouragement was as sexy as her body. Without conscious thought, he made quick work of the second and third buttons, kissing her through the silky fabric of her bra, teasing a hard nipple while he ran his thumb across the other one.

"Th-that feels so good," she panted.

For him, too. The only thing he could imagine that would feel better than touching her was being inside her again. He was on the brink of losing control? Make a last-ditch effort for rationality? Straightening, he searched her gaze. "If you want me to stop, now would be a good time to say so."

"Stop?" She sounded pained. "No, I… Is anyone home at the farm?"

He shook his head. His sister-in-law's family owned the place, but Kate's aunt was on a senior citizen gambling trip in Louisiana. "There's no one here to see us, if that's what you're worried about." When she glanced over his shoulder, he followed her gaze to the barn. "Want to go inside?"

She nodded without hesitation.

Jace paused only long enough to grab the blanket he kept in the back of his truck. "To give us a comfortable place to sit," he said, trying halfheartedly to sound innocent.

Layla gave him a slow, sexy smile. "And here I was thinking that sitting in your lap sounded like a good idea."

He groaned. "Woman, you are going to be the death of me."

Turning so that she was walking backward, she undid another button. "Complaining?"

"Hell, no." He scrambled to catch up with her, so eager that he nearly tripped over his own feet.

It was cool and dim inside the barn, with beams of light shining through the wood. The sweet smell of hay was nice but not nearly as intoxicating as the scent of Layla's skin or the shampoo she used. Could he really be this lucky?

"Are you sure about this?" he asked, barely recognizing his own voice. It was hoarse, scratchy with need and hope.

Her soft, reassuring laugh was the sweetest sound he'd ever heard. "Jace, I already had to seduce you once. Are you going to make me do it again, or will you just accept that I want you and do something about it?"

Chapter 11

Layla felt giddy with desire...and power. It was an amazing sensation to have such an effect on a big, strong cowboy like Jace Trent. But the power was a two-way street because that wicked grin he was giving her made her knees weak.

He tossed the blanket on the ground and advanced on her. "I've thought about this so many times, beautiful."

"Making out in a barn?" she teased.

"You know what I mean." Looking around, he suddenly laughed. "Although, we really should try a bed one of these days."

"Maybe another time." *Would* there be another time? Just what was she committing to here? After her talk with Gena last night, she'd fallen asleep with budding determination to go after what she wanted—namely, Jace. And when she'd shown up today to find him waiting for her… It felt as if she'd waited seven years for this moment, and she couldn't wait any longer.

He wrapped his arms around her, and they slid down to the blanket in a tangle of limbs and sighs. Her shirt was rapidly discarded, and his followed soon after. She experienced the briefest moment of shyness.

"I look different now," she said, aware that pregnancy and birth had changed her body.

"Yeah." His hands grazed lightly over her breasts, past her stomach and lower to her thighs. "You're even more beautiful than before." The hungry way he looked at her made his words more than empty flattery.

By brushing away her momentary insecurity, he left her free to enjoy this wholeheartedly. She reached for him, her fingers curling into the hard muscle of his back as they kissed. "You…are…" She managed a few breathless words. "*Such* a good kisser."

He grinned against her lips. "Thanks, but it's like dancing. You're only as good as your partner."

Then words were lost as he rolled her over, showing her with his every touch how much he wanted her. It had been quite a while since Layla had made love, but it had been far longer since she'd felt this soul-deep yearning. As nice as the foreplay was, she wanted him inside her. She wanted to feel that sense of completion.

"Jace." She couldn't wait any longer.

"I know."

"Do you, um, have protection?" She couldn't believe she hadn't remembered that before now, as cautious as she was about birth control, but her thoughts had been too full of him to register anything else.

He gave a short laugh. "What, you aren't on the Pill?" he teased.

After all these years of keeping the truth about her pregnancy from him, she couldn't believe they'd reached a place where they could joke about it. "Actually, I am. But I'd like to make extra sure. Just in case."

He pulled his wallet out of his back pocket, and she helped tug off his jeans. It was much easier to shimmy out of her shorts. She recalled how nervous she'd been last time they were in this position, but now there was only urgent joy. And an intimacy she wouldn't know how to put into words. This was the man who had given her the greatest gift she'd ever known, the person who had helped create their daughter. Whether Jace knew it or not, he'd been a part of her life every day since then. Feeling him slide into her now was like coming home. Or revisiting a miracle.

Her breath caught as he moved inside her, and she lifted her hips to his, arching to meet each thrust. He braced himself above her, his blue eyes intense with need.

"You're so beautiful," he whispered. For once, the word didn't sound like a casual habit. It sounded solemn. Reverent.

She met his gaze as long as she could, loving the connection. But then her muscles began to tighten, ripples of pleasure spreading through her. Her back bowed, and starbursts danced behind her eyelids. She cried out his name, hearing it echo through the barn as her body trembled. His own cries were nearly incoherent as he drove into her and found his own release.

When he collapsed above her, the barn fell silent, except for their harsh breathing. They sounded like two marathon runners who'd just made it past the finish line.

This is way more fun than running. A giggle erupted, and Jace poked her lightly in the ribs.

"This is no time to laugh at a guy." He rolled onto his side. "You'll give me a complex."

"I was just thinking that if all exercise was this fun, everyone would be in shape."

"Fun, huh?" He gave her a lazy smile. "Guess that's one word for what we just did."

She ran a hand through his hair, snuggling closer. "What would you have called it?"

"Perfect. The word I'd use is *perfect*."

"Wow." Gena's voice on the other end of the phone was both impressed and worried. "So you're really doing this?"

Layla flopped back on the guest room bed, second-guessing her decision. "You yourself said Addie needed to hear it from us before it was too late." After the day she'd spent badgering her stubborn father and brother to make peace with each other, telling them that this had gone on far too long, she'd been painfully reminded of her own situation. The time for Addie to know who her dad was had long passed. Tonight, she and Jace were going to fix that.

"Good luck."

"Thank you. I'm sorry that after all you've done for me, I'm repaying you by driving you out of your own home."

"I'm seeing a movie with a cute coworker. I'll survive."

"Have fun." *At least one of us should.* Layla would be spending her evening tense and nauseated.

After ending the call, Layla went to the kitchen where

Addie was doing the homework packet her teacher had emailed. "How's it going?"

Addie scowled. "I broke my green crayon."

"This might cheer you up. What if Jace brings over a pizza tonight?"

"Can it be pineapple and olives?"

"Yep. I already told him that was your favorite."

Her face lit up. "And we can watch that twisted movie!"

"*Twister*. But I don't think—"

"Can he teach me how to make a tornado machine?"

"Not tonight, honey. He has to buy special parts to make another one of those. But I know he's looking forward to making one with you. You can be patient, right?"

Her daughter groaned melodramatically.

Privately, Layla shared her daughter's opinion of waiting. The hour between telling Addie that Jace was coming for dinner and his arrival was excruciating. Layla didn't have any cooking to keep her busy, and although she could be working on the calendar, looking at the photos of Jace just made her more restless. She and Addie were on their third consecutive viewing of Dorothy's life in Kansas when the doorbell rang.

Layla shot to her feet. *This is it.* Tonight, she would tell her daughter the truth. She didn't just have a few butterflies in her stomach, she had an entire monarch migration.

When she opened the door, Jace smiled nervously, his expression a mirror of what she was feeling. Despite her trepidation, the sight of him sent happiness curling through her. "Hi," she said softly. "I'm glad you're here."

"Me, too."

"Pizza!" Addie skidded into the foyer in her sock-clad feet.

"Slow down before you plow into a wall," Layla warned.

"Or at least wear a crash helmet," Jace said.

Addie giggled, running over to hug Jace around the waist. Layla hoped her daughter was still willing to voluntarily dispense hugs by the end of the evening. Would she be angry? Shocked? Would she still trust her mom after this?

By unspoken agreement, neither Jace nor Layla brought up any heavy topics during dinner. They shared more stories about their adolescence with Chris and told Addie about the many town festivals in Cupid's Bow. The mayor had once jokingly called the town the Festival Capital of the Southwest. Addie happily chowed down on pizza, not seeming to notice that neither adult was hungry. Finally, though, Addie ran out of steam, picking a piece of pineapple off the half-eaten slice on her plate.

"Full?" Layla asked.

Addie nodded.

"You go wash your hands, and I'll clean up in here."

"Then we can watch *Twister*," her daughter suggested.

Layla almost chuckled. She supposed Addie's persistence was an inherited trait. After all, she had two stubborn parents. "Not tonight."

"Ooohkay." Addie stretched the first syllable out in protest, shuffling down the hallway in a pointedly dejected posture.

The minute Addie was out of sight, Jace grabbed Layla for a brief but heartfelt kiss. "I've been wanting to do that since you opened the door," he said.

She wished she could lose herself in his kisses long

enough to block out her growing anxiety, but it was time to face her past. She drew a shaky breath, trying to steady her nerves.

"Ready?" he asked.

"Hell, no." She conjured a smile.

"You've got this. *We've* got this."

How was the man still single? He was sympathetic and thoughtful and probably the best kisser in the Lone Star State. "I thought we should go in the living room where it's more comfortable. I don't want you to feel excluded, but it might be best if you let me do most of the talking."

He nodded. "Do you know what you're going to say?"

"I practiced three different versions this afternoon. But they all suck."

Addie came around the corner, rubbing her hands on her shirt. "What sucks?"

"Ah…that's probably not a word you should use," Layla said, imagining what the kindergarten teacher would think of her parenting skills. "It's more of a grown-up word."

"Like *damn*?" Addie asked.

Jace snorted with laughter. "Did you hear that from your mom, too?"

"No, Grandpa."

"How 'bout we go into the other room?" Layla suggested, trying to head off further conversation about interesting words Addie had overheard her grandfather use.

The three of them sat on the couch with Addie in the middle, and Layla thought fondly of the other night, when her daughter had fallen asleep against Jace. Watching father and daughter together, it was unthinkable that she'd ever planned to leave town again without him knowing the truth. Thank God he'd figured it out. She was on her way to finally being free of the guilt. She just had to share the truth with her loved ones. Starting with Addie.

She kissed the top of her daughter's head. "Honey, you know how I told you that you had a daddy I cared very much about a long time ago, but that he lived far away from us?"

"Uh-huh."

"Well." She swallowed. "This may be hard for you to understand, but Jace... We used to be best friends."

"Like me and Meredith."

"Um, sort of. The point is, he was very important to me. Then he moved away to go to college, and then *I* moved away and I didn't know he'd moved back to Cupid's Bow and I haven't seen him in a long time. And—"

"I'm your dad, Addie."

Layla's gaze jerked upward. She couldn't believe he'd blurted that out, but it wasn't as if she'd been doing such a stellar job with her explanation.

Addie frowned. "Mama, is he being silly?"

"No. Jace really is your father, but he didn't know for a long time, so please don't be mad at him for not visiting you or—"

"I'm sorry I missed your birthdays," Jace said. "I will buy you a present for every one of them I missed."

"Meredith's big sister says babies come from sex. Did you do sex to my mommy?"

"Uh…" He shot Layla a panicked look.

"It was a long time ago," Layla deflected. *And a couple of times yesterday.*

Addie looked mildly repulsed. "Did you two see each other naked? Is Jace going to live with us?"

"What? No, honey, but he is free to visit you as much as he—"

"Are you a policeman?"

Jace blinked.

"Meredith's dad is a policeman," Layla supplied, figuring that was Addie's closest frame of reference.

"I work at a store that sells cowboy gear," he told Addie.

"Some of the daddies come to my class and tell us about their jobs. Are you coming to my class? What's cowboy gear? Does your store have the stuff to make my tornado machine? How do you do sex? Can we watch *Twister*?"

"Yes," both adults chorused with varying degrees of desperation and relief.

Jace shot to his feet. "I'll go get the movie out of my truck."

While he left the room, Layla reached out to hug her daughter—slowly in case Addie wanted to pull away. "Are you okay, honey?"

"I'm hungry. Can we have popcorn?"

"Sure. But do you want to talk about Jace being your dad?"

"Are we a family now?"

A family. The word burned in Layla's chest. "Yes, but there are lots of different kinds of families. Not all of them live together."

"Can I have chocolate milk with my popcorn?" She'd definitely inherited Layla's taste for sweet-and-salty combinations.

"I'll be right back with it."

Jace came through the kitchen as Layla was making the popcorn. "How's she doing?"

"She seems to be taking it in stride? I've seen plenty of Addie meltdowns. When she's upset, she's not usually shy about expressing it. Maybe it hasn't sunk in yet, but I let her know that I'm available if she wants to talk and that we are both here for her."

"Which somehow translated to popcorn and chocolate?" he asked, grinning at the bottle of chocolate syrup on the kitchen counter.

She found herself grinning back. "Plus a movie I already said no to twice today. We may have been outsmarted by a six-year-old."

His face shone with fatherly pride. "That's my girl."

"You say that now, but the stakes are going to get a lot higher than a PG-13 movie and chocolate milk as she gets older."

"Then you and I better stick together. It's our only shot."

She squeezed his hand. "Welcome to the team."

Chapter 12

The only other time Jace had tucked his daughter into bed, she'd been asleep already. It turned out that the process wasn't as quick and easy when she was awake.

"Just one more story?" Addie begged, her eyes big.

He had so much lost time to make up for that it was on the tip of his tongue to say yes, but Layla cut him off. "That last story *was* your *one more*, remember?"

"But I—" Addie cocked her head, listening as the front door opened and closed. "Cousin Gena! I have to tell her good-night." Without giving either of them a chance to object, she scampered down off the bed, her voice echoing as she rushed down the hall.

"Cousin Gena, guess what? I saw a tornado movie with a *bunch* of tornados and a flying cow, but not really flying, and Jace is my dad."

His laugh was rueful. "At least I rate in the same sentence as the cow."

"Sounds like you three had an eventful night," Gena said as she walked Addie back to her room. She paused in the doorway, her expression questioning, asking without words if everything was okay.

Layla nodded almost imperceptibly.

Jace felt a rush of gratitude for the way the evening had gone. It was funny, how jealous he'd been of his brothers in recent weeks, because until tonight, he hadn't even understood how truly blessed they were. Something as simple as pizza and a movie with Layla and their daughter made him happy on a profound, soul-deep level. Had there really been a time when he'd balked at commitment? Trying to remember why was like trying to unimagine what colors looked like.

"Tonight was great," he told Gena. "Better than great."

"Can we do it again tomorrow?" Addie asked.

He beamed at her. "Y—"

Layla cleared her throat.

"You'll have to ask your mom," he amended. *"Please."*

"I don't think so," Layla said. "I have a pretty busy day tomorrow. But another time."

"Maybe next time, we can have dinner at my house," Jace offered. "If you're interested in seeing where I live."

"Sounds like a good idea," Layla agreed. "We'll do that soon."

"Promise?" Addie persisted.

Layla booped her daughter on the nose. "Only if *you* promise to hurry up and go to sleep."

Squeezing her eyes tightly shut, Addie yanked the blankets up to her chin and began to loudly "snore."

Jace stifled a laugh, trying not to encourage further antics—even if he did find them adorable.

"'Night, Addie Rose." Layla kissed the girl's forehead and left the room. Jace followed suit.

Gena had already made herself scarce. Jace grinned inwardly. Layla's cousin was a pro at silently disappearing. She could teach stealth to CIA operatives.

Alone with Layla in the hallway, he asked softly, "So, your schedule's pretty busy tomorrow?"

"Well, I'm meeting Quincy in the morn—"

He made an involuntary noise in his throat.

"What?" Layla frowned at him. "I thought you and Quincy were friends."

"Uh-huh. Hey, do you want me to come with you? Maybe I could help carry cameras or hold one of those light thingies or—"

"Jace Trent. Are you *jealous*?"

"Yup." He knew he didn't technically have any claim on Layla's affections, but he didn't care. Logical or not, he felt more possessive of her now than when she'd been a freshman and he'd wanted to deck any guy who looked at her the wrong way. He held his breath, wondering if she would angrily remind him that she was an independent woman who didn't answer to him.

Instead, she gave him a lopsided grin.

"You aren't mad?"

"No. I mean, I think you're ridiculous, obviously. But you're also…kind of sweet."

He could feel the answering grin on his face, knew he probably looked like a sappy fool. "Only kind of? Because I can try harder."

She giggled, a soft, musical sound that made his body tighten. She looked so purely happy, and knowing it was a reaction to him made him feel ten feet tall, like he could command the stars to twinkle brighter and stop a stampede with no more than a stern look.

"Walk me out to my truck?" he asked, his voice low with intent.

Her lips parted, her gaze shifting from amused to aroused.

"Damn, beautiful, it shouldn't be legal to look at a man like that."

She gave him a wicked grin. "Sorry, not sorry."

"Mama! Can I have a glass of water?"

Jace groaned.

Layla laughed, but there was frustration in her expression, too. "Parenting 101—expect interruptions at the worst possible times."

"I'm amazed my parents managed to have three of us."

"They must have really liked each other," she teased.

I like you. He didn't say it out loud because it was a ludicrous, seventh-grade declaration. But it was also the truth. Yesterday afternoon had proven that their sexual attraction was as strong as ever, but it was a lot more than that. He enjoyed her company, admired her, loved seeing her smile.

"Mama?"

"Coming," Layla called. To Jace, she said, "I'd better get that water. I'll see you out."

He followed her to the kitchen. "If your pictures with Quincy are in the morning, is there any chance of meeting you for a late lunch?"

"I'm not sure I could squeeze it in." She stood on tiptoe to get one of the kid-friendly plastic cups in the top of Gena's cabinet. Her shirt slid up over her stomach, and the glimpse of soft, creamy skin left him itching to touch her. "Tomorrow, Chris has an appointment with Sierra. My mom is driving him there, but she has a meeting in the afternoon, so I'm picking him up and taking him home."

"Another time?" He took the cup from her, tracing his thumb over the delicate skin of her wrist before moving away to the water dispenser. "I want to see you again." *Soon.*

She ducked her gaze, her cheeks rosy. "Well, obviously you'll see me again. You see me all the time."

It was funny, all the years that had passed when he *hadn't* seen her. He had friends and he'd found ways to stay busy over the past seven years, but with Layla back in town, he almost felt as if his life had been paused until now. His world was more vivid with her in it.

"Layla Dempsey, will you go on a date with me? A real one. I want to take you out to dinner and flirt with you while we wait for our food. I want to hold your hand walking down Main Street where anyone could see us."

"Oh. Jace, I don't know if…"

Disappointment curdled in his gut. Layla liked him enough to have sex with him in a barn, just not enough to have everyone in town know about it. "Never mind. Here." He handed her Addie's water. "Tell her I said sweet dreams, okay?"

"M-maybe you could meet me at Chris's?" Layla asked shyly. "I don't think tomorrow works for lunch or dinner, but we could fit in a milk shake. And, um, some hand-holding."

He wanted to pump his fist in the air and let out a triumphant whoop. But he was a grown man, and there was a little girl down the hall who was supposed to be getting sleepy. So he settled for giving Layla a huge grin and a brief kiss goodbye. "It's a date."

Feeling as though his feet weren't quite touching the ground, he stepped outside into the cool night air. He palmed his keys and climbed into his truck—where he drummed his hands against the steering wheel and let out the whoop of joy the occasion warranted.

When Layla entered the physical therapy gym, her brother looked the same way he had after his first junior rodeo win—sweaty and damned happy.

Sierra stood next to his wheelchair, coaxing him to try one final set of arm exercises. Well…not so much "coaxing" as bullying in the voice of a drill sergeant.

Chris gritted his teeth, his face a dark splotchy red, but he made it through four reps. With each one, Layla saw renewed determination in her brother's eyes.

"All right!" Sierra handed him a bottle of water. "Nice effort, Hot Wheels! I mean, I have a four-year-old patient who's a bigger badass than you, but give it time. I'll whip you into shape."

He grinned at her. "Does Jarrett realize he's married to a heartless monster?"

"It's one of the things he loves best about me." She brightened at the sight of Layla. "Hey! Good to see you again. Don't even *think* about leaving town before we've had the chance for a proper girls' night."

"Wouldn't dream of it," Layla promised.

Chris frowned. "I didn't realize you two were so well acquainted."

He had no idea Layla had spent a day on the Twisted R. It would be hard to explain until after he knew about the calendar. But Sierra covered with aplomb.

"Girls bond fast in hospital waiting rooms," she said with a shrug. "It was either get to know your sister or play Sudoku on my phone, and Layla was more interesting. After all, she knows stories about the dumb antics you and Jarrett and the others pulled when you were kids."

"Oh yeah?" Chris sent a warning glance in Layla's direction. "Don't forget—I know all the juicy stories about you, too."

Not all of them, big brother. She changed the subject. "Ready to go? Dad's waiting down in Suzanne's SUV."

Martin had wanted to be here in case she needed any help maneuvering Chris into the vehicle, but he'd said he hadn't felt right coming in with her. The two men had made some limited progress. Would they continue working on the estranged relationship after Martin headed home tomorrow? If nothing else, at least he'd had a chance to apologize for past mistakes in person and see with his own eyes that Chris was recovering after his accident.

But that didn't keep the ride to Chris's house from being awkward. The tension was thick, worse than the humidity off the coast in summer. Both men tried to solve the problem by directing their comments to Layla instead of conversing with each other.

"You sure you don't want me to take the pickle back with me?" Martin asked from the backseat. "I know you were worried about her missing so much school."

Layla hesitated. It had taken Addie weeks to adjust to the routine of her new school. Layla had voiced concerns to her dad that this disruption in schedule would undo all the progress they'd made. But now that Jace and Addie knew about each other, giving them time to bond seemed more important than drawing shapes and going over sight words Addie had known since she was four.

"Don't stress over school," Chris told Layla. "Your little girl is sharp as a tack. She'll catch up with no problem."

"I hope so." Layla told herself that Addie would have to readjust after the two-week winter break anyway. Thinking about Addie and Jace reminded Layla that she had a confession to make. *The first of many.* She cleared her throat. "On another topic, just so you know, Jace is meeting us at your house."

"Jace Trent?" Martin asked.

Chris snorted. "Of course, Jace Trent. Even you should know that—he's been my best friend since the dawn of time."

"Right. And your sister seemed pretty friendly with him, too."

Layla's gaze flew to meet her father's in the rearview mirror. How much did he know?

"When I ran into them at Gena's the other night—"

"Jace came to check on me," Layla interrupted her dad. "He's been a huge help. Bringing Mom soup when she was sick, inviting Addie and I to have dinner with his family when we first got here. I declined, but the offer was thoughtful. He's always been a good friend to our family."

Chris nodded. "I'm glad he's coming over. Maybe I can talk him into staying to watch the game later. We can crack open a couple of beers."

"With the number of medications you're on?" Layla challenged. "Not a chance, mister."

"Fine." Chris huffed out a sigh. "So we'll crack open a couple of root beers."

She hesitated. "Actually, one of the reasons he's meeting us there is to give me a ride. He and I have..." Plans? A date? "We're going to the diner to get milk shakes."

"Seriously?" Her brother laughed. "What are you, twelve?"

Instead of making jokes, her father leaned forward between the seats, studying her. "Is this a date, Layla Anne?"

"Yes." She gulped, cutting a sideways glance to check Chris's reaction.

"Wait... Like a date-date? My best friend asked out my kid sister without talking to me about it first?"

"In case you haven't noticed, I'm a grown woman with a kid and my own photo studio. I can drive a car and be out after dark and everything."

"Smartass," Chris said affectionately. "Well, at least Trent knows what he's getting with you. He won't be expecting some demure lady. He heard the way you swore when you got that fishhook caught in your finger. Hell, he's seen you yarf."

She grimaced. "Thanks for the reminder. Very romantic image."

"My best friend and my sister being romantic. Gross. On the other hand, if you actually started dating, you would have a reason to visit Cupid's Bow more. Suze and I would love that."

"Definitely something for me to consider," she said as they turned onto Chris's street. All in all, her brother had taken the news quite well—not that meeting for milk shakes in broad daylight was all that scandalous. Still, this was a good omen.

Eager to hear about Chris's PT session, Suzanne met them in the driveway, a baby monitor receiver sticking out of her skirt pocket. She made sure to include Martin in her warm smile of greeting. Layla was confident that her sister-in-law would do all that she could to help facilitate the family peace.

"I feel like a bad lightbulb joke," Chris grumbled. "How many people does it take to get one me into the house?"

"If it will make you feel like less of an invalid," Suzanne offered, "I can sit in your lap. Wanna give me a ride?"

He waggled his eyebrows. "Definitely."

Layla made gagging sounds. "Yuck."

"Oh!" Chris clapped his hands together. "That reminds me…you'll never believe who Lay-la has a daaate with." He made the words singsong, like a nine-year-old on the playground. Any minute now, he was going to tell everyone she and Jace had been K-I-S-S-I-N-G.

"A date?" Suzanne looked delighted. "That's wonderful."

"We're just getting milk shakes," Layla mumbled.

"With Jace Trent," Chris said. "My little sister canoodling with the guy who showed me how to unhook a bra. Forget physical therapy, I may need therapy therapy. Speak of the devil…"

Layla knew that if she turned around, she'd see Jace's truck pulling in behind them. She was already blushing so hard that it was probably visible from space. The idea of greeting him with her father, brother and sister-in-law watching made her regret telling Chris about the date in the first place.

The truck door opened and closed. "We having some kind of tailgate party?" Jace asked. "If I'd known, I would've brought chips."

Chris snorted. "We wouldn't want to keep you from the diner."

Layla glanced over her shoulder, happiness buzzing through her when Jace met her gaze. "I, um, told him about our date."

He beamed. "Good." He crossed the distance between them in a couple of long strides, framed her face with his hands and leaned in to kiss her hello.

"Ugh. It's worse than I imagined," Chris heckled, just as Martin added, "I did not need to see that."

Layla grinned. "You'll have to forgive my family. They think they're funny." In a whisper, she added, "What the hell is this I hear about you teaching my brother to unhook a bra?"

Jace looked upward, his expression all innocence. "So... How was the therapy session with Sierra?"

"Come on inside," Suzanne invited, "and Chris can tell us all about it. I haven't got the update yet, either."

"Sounds good." Jace dropped his arm around Layla's shoulders as if it were the most natural thing in the world, and she couldn't resist cuddling closer against him.

From the corner of her eye, she saw her dad smile. When she turned in his direction, he mouthed, *Good for you*. In the past six years, Martin had spent more time with her than anyone else here, and he knew how rarely she dated. Did her dad ever worry about her being lonely? He certainly hadn't seemed sorry to see Kyle go; Addie wasn't the only one who'd disliked her would-be boyfriend.

Inside the house, Jace and Martin got Chris situated in the living room while Layla grabbed a stack of cups and a pitcher of lemonade. Suzanne peeked into the nursery to make sure the twins were still napping peacefully. When Layla rejoined the men, she was happy to discover that they were talking about fishing, one of the hobbies her brother and father had shared before they stopped speaking. She would never be glad that her brother had been in such a terrible accident, but if it brought Chris and their dad closer together, then at least something good had come from it. *Not to mention that it reunited you and Jace.*

"Did I miss anything?" Suzanne asked as she entered the room.

Chris shook his head. "No, I—"

Outside, a car door slammed.

"You guys expecting anyone?" Layla asked.

Her sister-in-law shrugged. "Lots of folks have been dropping by since Chris got home from the hospital. They've kept our freezer so full of casseroles and lasagnas, all I have to do lately to prepare dinner is press—"

The front door flew open. "So it *is* true!" Claire marched into the room, eyes wide, voice shaking. Her infuriated gaze zeroed in on Martin. "I cannot believe this. My family's been lying to me, and I had to hear it as secondhand gossip from someone in town? Just like old times, isn't it, Marty? Once again, you've made me look like a fool!"

Martin shot an apologetic glance at Layla, and she knew what he was thinking. If he'd just left one day sooner, they could have avoided this. *Or, if Mom and Dad had talked through their differences like civilized human beings* years ago, *that might have prevented the problem, too.*

"Now, Mama." Chris kept his voice low, either to soothe his mother's temper or to avoid waking the girls.

"It's not like this was some big conspiracy. Dad just brought Layla a couple of things for her extended stay. I didn't even know he was in town until Layla—"

"You!" Claire's head whipped toward her daughter. "I should have known. You always find a way to team up with him against me."

Layla's stomach knotted. She was six years old again, the unworthy sibling, the one who always disappointed her mom. Should she have told Claire outright that Martin was in town? She'd been trying to avoid a scenario just like this, but maybe it was time to start standing up to her mom, to face her family's problems directly.

"And after I bared my soul to you," Claire continued, shaking a finger at Layla. "To think, I asked you to move back! I wanted—"

"Don't you take this out on her," Martin interjected. "The problems between us are *between us*."

"Stay out of it," Claire retorted. "I was talking to my daughter, not you."

This was awful. It was like the countless screaming matches Layla had endured in the months before the divorce was final. As a teenager, her preoccupation with Jace and his friendship were what got her through the worst of it. Now she reached blindly for his hand, and he squeezed her fingers in his, letting her know she wasn't alone.

"Oh, so now she's your daughter?" Martin challenged. "The one you couldn't be bothered to check on while she was in labor? The one you hardly call unless you feel like guilt-tripping her? Lord, no wonder she rarely visits you, Claire. You—"

"How dare you!" his ex-wife yelled. "You don't get to judge me, you adulterous, deceitful—"

Down the hall, a baby began crying, and Suzanne groaned.

"Enough!" Chris thundered. "Do you see what you people did? You woke one of the—"

A second infant joined the first.

Chris and Martin both swore, father and son mirror images of each other. Claire ignored them both, shrieking at Layla about ungrateful daughters.

"So." Jace loudly cleared his throat. "Did Layla happen to mention that I'm Addie's father?"

The living room fell into shocked silence. Even the twins were quieting now that Suzanne had reached them. All eyes turned to Layla, but for one blessed second, her family was speechless. She could finally hear herself think.

She eyed Jace, nearly as stunned by his announcement as everyone else. "Thanks. I think."

Chapter 13

Admittedly, Jace hadn't done much mental analysis before lobbing his verbal grenade into the middle of the room. Instead, he'd reacted on instinct, spurred by the increasing panic on Layla's face. He'd always known Claire disapproved of her daughter's teenage pregnancy, and it had occurred to him as Claire lashed out that *he* was partly responsible for the rift between mother and daughter. So he'd offered himself up as a potential target, hoping to deflect attention from the pale woman who'd had his hand in a death grip. Now, Layla's parents and brother were staring at him with murder in their eyes, and he wasn't entirely sure whether Layla herself wanted to throttle him.

On the other hand, at least the secret was out. So, if he lived through this, he could finally tell his family about Addie.

Chris spoke through gritted teeth. "What the hell do you mean you're Addie's father?"

Jace tightened his hold on Layla, subtly putting himself between her and her family. "Exactly what I said," he said evenly. "And I understand if you're ticked at me, man, but I will not apologize for being part of the reason Addie Rose is in this world. She's a great kid."

Chris opened his mouth, then closed it again, unable to argue that.

Claire Brewer was not as willing to let him off the hook. "You seduced my daughter? After all the times I welcomed you into my home, and—"

"Mom, you've got it backward. I, uh… The whole thing was—"

"Mutual," Jace said quickly. "It was also years ago, so we're just going to have to move past it like adults. And I'm sorry to have announced it in such a tactless way, but Layla already told me her dad is leaving town in the morning. It's been what, seven years since you've all been in the same room together? So I impulsively seized this rare opportunity to tell you something Layla has been dying to get off her chest. I'm sure she would have told you sooner if she hadn't been worried about people yelling and screaming and generally losing their shit."

Claire's face was red, and he could tell she wanted to yell at him for his not-so-subtle dig, but since that would just prove his point, she pursed her lips and contented herself with glaring daggers.

Martin, on the other hand, stepped forward. "You got my daughter pregnant and didn't do a blasted thing to help her until now?"

"Daddy, he didn't even know. I didn't want to derail

Jace's life just as he was headed off to college, and I was half-afraid our families would make us get married—"

"Damn straight."

"—and I was terrified he'd end up hating me. Like you and Mom hate each other. That's the last thing I wanted."

Martin drew back a little, deflated. "I don't hate your mama."

"Well, *I*—"

"Really, Mom?" Chris chided gently. "Maybe, right at this exact second, it shouldn't be about you." He narrowed his gaze on Jace. "You're my best friend. You should have told me. Not about being Addie's father," he clarified when both Layla and Jace started to point out that Jace hadn't been aware. "About you and Layla, period. The two of you were together *seven years ago*, and the first I'm hearing of it is her casual mention that you're grabbing a milk shake today? Not cool."

Jace hung his head. That was really the only part he felt guilty for, jeopardizing his friendship with Chris. But there was no good way to tell a buddy you'd deflowered his sister. "Sorry, man."

"You shouldn't have to say you're sorry to any of them," Layla said. "What happened between us is our business. And, well, Addie's, but we took care of that last night." She pinched the bridge of her nose, looking exhausted. "Frankly, I could really use that promised milk shake now. So if you guys want to continue the shouting match, feel free, but I'm going. Jace?"

"Yes, ma'am." To the room at large, he said, "I'm with her. But if any of you want to scream at me later, you know where to find me."

He followed Layla outside, fully expecting her to

read him the riot act once they were alone. She'd kept this secret for years, and he hadn't managed to keep his mouth shut about it for more than a few days. He wasn't sorry that people knew. Hell, he wanted to shout from the top of the Cupid's Bow water tower with a bullhorn that Addie was his. But he was willing to listen if Layla needed to vent her feelings. She could be fierce, but she'd never been able to stay angry for long.

Taking a deep breath, he closed the door behind him and braced himself.

Layla turned around—and smiled. "Well. That was weird."

"A little bit. You aren't upset?"

"Oh, I'm definitely upset. Poor Chris and Suzanne had enough on their plates already without my parents bringing in all of their drama and me adding to it. And I think it's nuts that Mom and Dad still get under each other's skin like that. Who holds a grudge that long? But... I feel relieved, too." She smiled as he opened the passenger-side door for her. "When I found out I was pregnant, I was so scared of how everyone would react when they learned the truth. That fear never truly left me until just now. I mean, you definitely had no right to do that, but everyone else was acting foolish, so I guess, when in Rome..."

"I hated how your mom was talking to you. I wanted to do something to draw her fire away from you."

"And that was the only idea you had for a distraction? What, you don't know any knock-knock jokes?"

"For you, beautiful, I'll learn some."

Jace hadn't realized it until after he and Layla were shown to their table, but today was the first time he'd been back to the diner since he'd learned the truth about Addie. That day had ended with Layla fleeing in tears. Thankfully, this afternoon's visit ended with them strolling down Main Street to meet up with Gena at the bank. Layla's cousin had dropped her off earlier to pick up Suzanne's SUV, which was a better accommodation for Chris than Layla's compact car.

Just like in Jace's daydream, he and Layla were walking hand in hand, and it was ridiculous how happy such a simple touch made him. The only thing that marred his good mood was realizing how soon Layla and Addie would be leaving. The calendar was almost finished, and Chris was healing.

"Hey," he said, "I wanted to ask about something your mom said."

"Fire away, but I'm not sure I can answer questions about that woman without a psych degree."

"Did she really ask you to move back to Cupid's Bow?"

"Yeah, she did. And today reminded me why that would be a terrible idea. Thank goodness Addie spent today playing with Skyler. I don't know how I would have explained all of that drama to her if she'd witnessed it. She needs stability in her life, not outbursts."

He could understand why Layla wasn't in a hurry to move closer to her mother, but what about all of the other amiable citizens in town? Like Chris and Suzanne. Jarrett and Sierra. *Me.* He wanted to press the issue, but she'd already had an emotionally draining afternoon. Was now the best time to suggest she uproot her life when their relationship status was somewhere between barn hookup and milk shake date?

The milk shakes had been rich and thick and delicious…but not nearly as sweet as kissing Layla good-bye in full view of anyone in the general vicinity of the bank. This was how they were supposed to be—not some shameful secret kept from others, but a couple unafraid to express affection and attraction. *A couple.* That should be their relationship status.

Dropping his hands to her waist, he leaned back to meet her eyes. "I think I'm falling for you, Layla Dempsey."

She blinked up at him, looking confused for a split second, and then her lips curved into a smile that out-shone the sun. "Really?"

"You even have to ask?"

Grabbing him by the front of the shirt, she pulled him close for another kiss, this one deeper and hungrier. They were both breathless when they broke apart again. She giggled. "If I had a time machine, I would go back and tell my sixteen-year-old self about this. She would *freak*."

He grinned. "Sorry it took me so long to catch up." He'd do his best to make sure he'd been worth the wait. "See you and Addie tomorrow?" He'd invited them over and was excited for his daughter to see him home.

"We'll be there." She gave him one more kiss, then turned to head into the bank. On the second step, she paused and looked back at him. "Jace? I'm falling for you, too. In case that, ah, wasn't clear."

He was still grinning like a lovestruck fool when he reached the public parking lot two blocks later. But his jubilant mood dipped slightly at the sight of Will lean-ing against his truck, wearing his firefighter uniform and a grim expression.

"Hey, bro. What are you doing here? Everything okay with Megan and the girls?"

"No. I saw your truck from the station and was hoping if I waited a little bit, I could give you a heads-up. You weren't answering your phone."

He'd had it on Silent during his date with Layla. Now he pulled it out of his pocket and saw that his mother had called. Seven times. So had Will and Cole. And Chris.

Will stared him down. "Tell me you did not actually knock up little Layla Dempsey."

So much for being the one to tell his family.

There was not enough aspirin in the world for the amount of yelling Jace had endured today. First, it had been Layla's family. But for the past hour, it had been his own parents—his father glaring in disapproval from across the dining room table while Jace's mom paced back and forth in front of the china cabinet.

Apparently, Claire Brewer had exacted her revenge by leaving a message for Jace's mother. Will had escorted Jace to the subsequent emergency family meeting while Megan stayed home with their three little girls. Cole and Kate were already there, trying to calm an uncharacteristically hysterical Gayle Trent. The minute Jace had walked in the door, his parents had ambushed him, both talking at once, which was rare. Normally, his quieter father let Gayle speak for both of them. At first, they'd been hurt and confused about why Jace had never mentioned to them that he had a child. It was necessary to tell them that he hadn't known until now, but the last thing he wanted was for them to be angry with Layla. In his attempt to make her situation sympathetic, he'd played up how young and scared she'd been…which only agitated his parents further.

"I cannot believe you had sex with that girl," his mother wailed. "She was a *teenager.*"

"So was I."

"Exactly my point." She tossed her hands above her head. "You were barely out of high school, definitely not responsible enough to become a father!"

Harvey Trent scowled at his youngest son. "It didn't occur to you to keep it in your pants?"

Patience beginning to fray, Jace muttered, "Like I'm the only one here who didn't start college a virgin."

Cole promptly smacked him on the back of the head. "This isn't about us." Under his breath, he added, "And I'm pretty sure both Will and I gave you the condom talk. But you never were a good listener."

On the other side of Cole, his wife Kate tried to disguise a smothered laugh as a cough.

"Mom," Will interrupted, "would you consider sitting down for a second? You're making me dizzy. And with the way you keep waving your hands around, you might break something."

Gayle paused midpace. "Are you telling your own mother what to do?"

"No, ma'am, merely making a suggestion based on the common sense you worked so hard to instill in your sons."

She harrumphed at him but took a seat.

Having gained momentary control of the situation, Will tried to head off any more lecturing from their parents. "We all have questions for Jace, but this might work better if we actually give him a chance to answer."

Jace glanced at his brother, wordlessly expressing his gratitude. He definitely owed Will a beer in exchange for his diplomacy. "I know you're all shocked. To say *I* was shocked would be a gross understatement. I wanted to tell you all immediately, but Layla asked me to wait a few days. Her family has been through so much with Chris's accident, and I wanted to respect her wishes. You went six years without knowing, so what would a couple more days hurt? It's not ideal that she kept Addie a secret from me, but as you pointed out, Mom, I would have been terrible at handling that responsibility at the time. So I forgive Layla for keeping it to herself." And he hoped they would, too. Anyone who had a problem with her had a problem with him.

"All of that is in the past," he added. "Irrelevant now. What's important is my daughter—your granddaughter, your niece. Addie is smart and beautiful and sweet. She has Layla's curly hair, and she wants to be a meteorologist when she grows up. Layla says Addie is already one of the best readers in her kindergarten class. I can't wait for her to meet all of you." As he finished, he became aware that his entire family was staring at him. Not merely looking at him, paying attention as he spoke, but gawking at him in various expressions of wonder and curiosity. He resisted the urge to pat his shoulder and make sure he hadn't sprouted a second head. "What?"

It was Kate who spoke first. "You're absolutely in love with her, aren't you?"

He wasn't sure whether she meant Addie or Layla, but it was equally true for both of them.

Kate sighed happily. "Jace Trent, family man… Never thought I'd see the day."

He ducked his head, suddenly self-conscious. "Is it really that big a stretch of the imagination? Both my brothers managed to find women to put up with them. Why not me?"

Gayle cleared her throat, drawing his attention. Her eyes glimmered with tears, but other than that, she looked calm for the first time since he'd set foot in the house. "Do you have pictures of my grandbaby?"

Nodding, he pulled up his favorites that Layla had texted him and passed the phone across the table to his parents. Harvey leaned close to his wife, while Cole, Will and Kate crowded behind them to peer over their shoulders.

Gayle sniffled, but she was smiling when she met Jace's eyes. "She has your eyes. You'll be bringing her to meet us soon." It was not a question.

"If you all promise to stop yelling."

"Deal," Gayle said. "We'll have Layla and Addie over for dinner, just as soon as it's convenient for them. Find out Addie's favorite dessert."

"Okay, but if I can make a suggestion, you might also want to brush up on trivia facts about tornados between now and then."

Cole snapped his fingers. "I think I actually have a few informational brochures at the station! Strictly speaking, tornados aren't police business, but the county did a series on general preparedness two years ago."

Rounding the table to give Jace his phone back, Will nodded. "The fire department is a major part of any poststorm ICS. We have the right tools to help get to victims, as well as the PPE— Oh, that's personal protective equipment," he said for the civilians at the table.

At the reminder that both of his brothers were employed full-time in emergency services, Jace groaned inwardly. Addie was going to end up liking her uncles more than her dad. Then again, he did have an idea for something special he could do for his daughter. And now would be a perfect time to enlist some much-needed help.

"I know this is short notice, but could I get you guys to lend me a hand with a big surprise?"

Will smacked him on the back of the head; it was amazing Jace didn't have a permanent dent there, courtesy of his brothers. "I think this family has had about all the surprises it can handle for one day."

"Think of it as a...welcome gift. And we have just over twenty-four hours to pull it together."

It was a good thing Layla already knew her way to Jace's house and didn't have to concentrate on following directions. With Addie's nonstop, mile-a-minute chatter from the backseat, they might have ended up hopelessly lost, circling Cupid's Bow until Layla ran out of gas. Her daughter was obviously very excited to learn how to make her own tornado machine.

"Did you know Skyler has *two* daddies? One lives with her at the house next to Gena, but sometimes she lives with the other one. I only need one daddy. When can we watch the flying cow movie again?"

Layla grinned at that. The "flying cow" movie had become an instant favorite. Although Layla had been concerned it might be too intense for her daughter, she had to admit it was nice to have a break from *The Wizard of Oz*.

"We're here," Layla declared. She'd asked Suzanne to look through some of Chris's old pictures so that she could show Addie photos of Jace's house before bringing her to visit. Her daughter had been fascinated by the images of Jace and Layla as kids.

Layla had made copies of the best in the bunch. Not

only did she want Addie to have them as keepsakes, Layla had also decided to put together a small surprise for Jace. It wasn't ready yet, but it shouldn't take long, especially since she'd taken the last of the calendar photos today. The final project would be delivered to Mona Stapleton for production by this weekend. *And then what?* Layla had a studio to run, and Addie should get back to school.

Don't get maudlin. Sure, long-distance dating was inconvenient, but it wasn't impossible. There were all kinds of tools they could use to build their relationship and stay in touch, from smartphones to texting to computer cameras. Jace had told her yesterday that he was falling for her. After years of complicated history, they might have an actual future together. It would just take time and patience. And if he lost interest? Well...better to know sooner rather than later.

She tried to shake off the worry. If Gena were here, she'd be telling Layla not to borrow trouble. Resolving to be more optimistic, she knocked on the front door. Jace answered within moments, looking sexier than he had a right to with his rumpled hair and a wooden kitchen spoon in his hand, barefoot in a pair of jeans and a Cupid's Bow Centennial T-shirt.

"My favorite two ladies!" He hugged Addie. "I was just telling my mom how wonderful you are, and she can't wait to meet you. In fact, she sent you a present."

"She did?" Addie looked as if she wasn't sure what to do with this information.

Layla kicked herself for not thinking to pull out pictures of Jace's family. In addition to showing Addie where he lived, Layla could have already started "introducing" her daughter to her new relatives.

The three of them filed into Jace's house. He had neatly lined up the pieces and parts needed for the tornado machine, along with a hot glue gun not yet plugged in. Addie's eyes lit up in anticipation of their project.

"Before we get busy with this," Jace said, "can I give you the present from my mom?"

Addie glanced from the tornado kit to Jace, grappling with her manners. "Okay."

Jace disappeared around the corner to pull a wrapped package out of the closet. It was a sizable rectangle, bigger than the sixteen-by-twenty canvas portraits popular with Layla's clients. Layla watched with curiosity as her daughter tore through the shiny pink paper.

Once she realized what she was holding, Addie gasped. "This is like what my teacher has!"

Tilting her head to get a better look, Layla saw that her daughter was holding a wood-frame magnetic calendar. It was the kind where kids used magnets to mark what day of the week it was, the date, the season and—best of all—the current weather conditions. Options included a smiling sun, a thunderbolt surrounded by raindrops, a snowflake and a cloud with a face, its lips pursed and blowing a strong gust of wind.

"That is from your grandma Gayle and grandpa Harvey. They were very excited for you to have it," Jace said.

Layla wanted to kiss him. "I'll bet they had a little help picking that out."

He met her gaze over Addie's head. "Maybe just a bit." To his daughter, he said, "That's just one part of your present."

"There's more?" Addie asked.

"Well, we have to decide what to do with the calendar. You can take it with you, but you might also want to hang it up." He turned toward the hallway, motioning for them to follow.

Layla tried not to sigh as they passed the master bedroom. She and Jace still hadn't made it to a bed. They really needed to rectify that.

Across from the master bedroom, there was a smaller room she vaguely remembered as his grandmother's sewing room. But as Jace flipped on the light switch, Layla saw that the room had been dramatically updated.

The furniture was simple—a modest bookshelf, a dresser and a bed. But the comforter on the bed was white, covered in rainbows, and a stuffed teddy bear sat at the foot of the bed, dressed in a yellow raincoat and galoshes. There were two pillows at the top of the bed. One was blue with a fluffy white cartoon cloud; the other was dark gray with a smiling thundercloud. The ceiling fan had a yellow dome light fixture and yellow blades, so that it looked like a sun in the middle of the room. The most thoughtful touch was that someone had stenciled a small black-and-green tornado with a friendly, mischievous face on the wall above the bookshelf.

"Ta-da!" Jace beamed at Addie. "What do you think? You can hang up your calendar here, but it's okay if you would rather—"

The calendar fell to the ground, magnets scattering on the floor. Addie turned to Layla wild-eyed. "Do I hafta live in two places like Skyler? Am I moving?"

"Oh!" Jace knelt down to be on eye level with his daughter, his expression so chagrined that Layla's heart hurt for him. "No. You're not moving. I didn't mean to worry you. I just thought…you might like to visit sometime."

"Like a sleepover?" Addie asked stiffly. She'd previously refused sleepover invitations from both Meredith and Skyler. It was clear from her frozen posture that she wouldn't relish one here, either. "Without Mommy?"

"Uh…" He sent Layla a pleading look. "Your mom is welcome to stay, too. You don't even have to sleep here. You could just play in this room. We could read stories together. Or…"

"I like this room!" Layla declared brightly. She wrapped her arms around the teddy bear and flopped down on the bed. "Man, this mattress is comfortable."

Addie met her gaze. "It is?"

"Absolutely." Layla patted the mattress next to her. "Want to come see?"

She took a hesitant step forward.

"Want an airplane ride?" Jace asked, holding his arms out. "You can go flying onto the bed."

Finally, Addie smiled. "Like the cow?" She reached for Jace, and he scooped her up, zooming her around the room in a circle before landing her next to Layla.

He stretched out on the other side of Addie, grinning with relief. Layla smiled back. *I finally got him in a bed.* Of course, this wasn't how she'd planned it, but single parents were nothing if not adaptable.

"I am so, so sorry about that," Jace whispered, barely audible over the popcorn in the microwave. Addie had gone to get the rainy-day bear to watch *Twister* with them. "The very last thing I wanted to do was upset her."

Layla rubbed his shoulder. "I know that."

"I just wanted to give her a space in my house that was hers alone. I had no idea it would scare her."

"Jace. I *know*." On the one hand, it would've been great if he'd given Layla a heads-up about what he'd planned. Traditionally, Addie did not do well with surprises. Still, Layla could appreciate his impulse to do something special for his daughter after all of the birthdays and Christmases that he'd missed. "She's okay now that we've reassured her she's not getting relocated. And none of the calendar pieces broke. So no harm, no foul. It really is a lovely room. How long have you been working on that?"

"Since last night," he said, looking boyishly pleased with himself.

She thought of the ceiling fan that had been installed and the wall stencil, the carefully chosen comforter set and perfect teddy bear. "You did that all in less than a day?"

"It helps to have a big family. And a mom who's friends with the owner of the local toy store."

She shook her head at him. "You really are something else, Jace Trent."

He stepped closer, his hand sliding over the curve of her hip. "Would this be a smart time for me to ask a favor?"

"Definitely."

"Before you leave town, what are the odds I could invite *you* for a sleepover, beautiful?"

She shivered in anticipation. "Play your cards right, and not only will I sleep over sometime soon, I'll leave my pajamas at home."

Chapter 14

"All done." Layla sat back in the chair, sighing at her laptop.

Gena leaned against the kitchen counter. "Don't people usually sound happier about successfully completing projects? If you didn't have plans with the Trents tonight, I'd say we should go do something to celebrate."

The calendar files were on their way to Mona, and soon she and Chris's friends would be able to tell him about their attempt to raise a little cash for him and Suzanne. She was looking forward to it, could already imagine the amused smirk on Chris's face when he saw the half-dressed photos of his closest buddies. *And then it will be time to go.*

Past time, really. Earlier today, when Skyler had asked if Addie wanted to come over, Addie had turned the offer down, then complained that she missed Meredith.

And her class. And her bed at home. Layla understood. Gena's hospitality was second to none—her cousin had been an amazing source of support—but eventually you got antsy staying under someone else's roof.

Really, the only downside of leaving Cupid's Bow was leaving Jace behind, but they had plans for their grown-up sleepover tomorrow, so it would be a good opportunity for them to have an uninterrupted discussion about the future. She would feel better once they'd reaffirmed their commitment to making this work. All that was needed was a little give and take from both parties. *Cheer up—you have a career you love and a daughter who is your world, plus the only man you've ever loved might just love you back.* She should feel victorious.

She rubbed her forehead with the heel of her hand. "Maybe I'm just tired. Or nervous about facing Jace's parents tonight." She'd always gotten along well with the Trents...but that was before she seduced their son, secretly had his baby and lied to everyone about it. "You don't think they hold a grudge, do you?"

"You gave them a beautiful grandbaby, and they're going to adore her—and, by extension, you. Plus, Jace is nuts about you. He wouldn't let you walk unknowingly into a bad situation." Gena chuckled. "I still can't believe he took on your mom, who called by the way."

"What?"

"She called the house phone while you were in the shower. I think she doubted you'd answer your cell if you saw it was her. I was waiting until you finished with the calendar to give you the message because I know talking to her can be a little—"

"Maddening? Crazy-making? Counterproductive?"

"Distracting. If you want to call her back, I can go make sure that Addie is getting ready."

Layla's daughter had been quietly sculpting clay animals, which was a good way to spend an hour or two. But Layla would prefer that Addie didn't meet her grandparents for the first time with orange-and-blue clay tangled in her curls. "Better yet, *I'll* check on Addie, and *you* call my mom. Just pretend to be me. She and I don't talk much, so she probably wouldn't recognize my voice anyway."

Flashing her a sympathetic grin, Gena left the kitchen, calling over her shoulder, "Wine's in the fridge if you need it."

Ha! Like Layla would risk showing up tipsy for dinner with the Trents? Besides, not even wine could dull the pain of talking to Claire. That might require hospital-grade sedation.

As Layla scrolled through her contacts list, she realized she hadn't asked Gena what Claire was calling about. *Oh, probably just the usual—disapproval, disgust and diatribes.* She gritted her teeth as the phone rang. Maybe she'd catch a break, and the call would go to voice mail.

"Layla Anne?"

"Hi, Mom."

"I wasn't sure Gena gave you my message. I called quite some time ago." Translation: *What took you so long*?

"Well, it's been a busy day. I was finishing up that project I told you about for Chris, and Jace will be picking up me and Addie soon. She's meeting her other grandparents tonight."

There was a tense silence. "I'm sure they'll be better grandparents than I am."

Layla wasn't sure how to interpret that. Not too long ago, Claire had surprised her by praising Layla's mothering skills—only to turn around minutes later and lambaste her for being an ingrate who refused to drop everything and move back to Cupid's Bow when summoned. This could be a trap. "I don't know what kind of grandparents they'll be," she said neutrally.

"They raised good men," Claire said. "I'm glad Addie is the daughter of Jace Trent and not some drunken stranger you met at a high school party. And I...understand now why you left town the way you did. I'd like to put all of that behind us."

"So would I, Mom. But honestly? I'm not sure we can until you put all of the stuff with Dad behind you. I don't expect you to be friends with him—"

Claire made a guttural, snarling sound.

"But if you want to be part of my life or Addie's life, you have to learn how to be in a room with him for ten minutes without screaming at anyone. It's not my fault or Chris's fault that the two of you got divorced, but we're both paying for it. And so are our kids. They should be able to know *all* of their grandparents, not be born into having to choose sides." Hearing the words come out of her own mouth, Layla was a little impressed. She'd never had the courage to say all of that to Claire before. This trip to Cupid's Bow had made her stronger.

"I'll work on it," Claire said, "but it will take time."

Layla bit back the reminder that time had already passed—years and years, in fact. She'd made the point she wanted to make and didn't have time for bickering. So she simply told her mom she'd see her at Chris's for dinner in a few days. The timing should work out that Layla would have the first box of calendars by then.

By the time Layla got off the phone, there were only about ten minutes left before Jace arrived. She was already wearing the sweater and long brown leather skirt she'd picked out for dinner; it was an attractive but appropriately modest outfit. She took a moment to touch up her makeup and pull her hair into a bouncy ponytail, then went to check on Addie.

Her daughter was presentable and clay-free, missing only her shoes.

"Can I bring my bear with me?" Addie asked as Layla searched under the bed for Addie's left sneaker.

"Absolutely. It's a good way to let Jace know you like his present." Layla stood up, trying to decide on the next logical place to look since she hadn't located the shoe yet.

"Will there be more presents?"

Now that Layla thought about it, Jace had given his daughter something practically every time he saw her. Layla needed to gently discourage that before he unintentionally spoiled Addie rotten. "No, honey. I don't think so." Except for one small gift that Layla had cobbled together for Jace. "Where was the last place you remember having your shoe?"

"On my foot."

The doorbell rang, and Layla glanced down to make sure she didn't have carpet lint on her skirt. "Okay, you keep looking, and I'll be right back." Her pulse did the flutter of anticipation that had become usual when she saw Jace; she was beginning to think of it as his own personal drumroll.

But Gena had beaten Layla to the door. Layla heard

their voices in the kitchen and her cousin telling Jace, "She'll be right here. Help yourself to a glass of water or sweet tea while you wait." Then she turned the corner, passing Layla in the hallway.

Gena fanned herself and silently mouthed the word, *"Wow."*

When Layla got to the kitchen, she saw what her cousin had meant. Wow, indeed. Layla's shirtless cowboy had been temporarily replaced by a *GQ* model. It was difficult to say which look was hotter. Jace was wearing dark slacks that looked tailor-made for his body and a deep blue dress shirt that made his eyes even more mesmerizing. It was sweet that he'd replaced his typical T-shirt and jeans for the evening; obviously, he considered introducing Addie to his parents a special occasion.

"Am I underdressed?" she asked. "I mean, you look amazing."

"Thank you." He wrapped a finger in one of the loose tendrils that framed her face and tugged lightly. "So do you. Where's Addie?"

"Hunting for her missing shoe."

He took full advantage of the delay, backing her against the wall until his body was pressed into hers. She was grateful for the wall's support in keeping her upright, because when Jace kissed her, her knees went weak. His hands slid just under the hem of her sweater, grazing her skin as he teased her sensitive lower lip and explored her mouth with his. Shivers ran along her body when he moved to her earlobe.

"I like your hair up like this," he said. "Easy access."

She tried not to moan at the decadent sensations he was stirring. "I like what you're doing." She knew they'd smeared her lip gloss, knew they were running the risk of getting caught, but she couldn't bring herself to care, not when light and heat and need were pulsing through her in time with Jace's heartbeat.

"I can't wait until tomorrow night," he told her. "I'm going to kiss you for hours. Everywhere."

She did moan then. Tomorrow night seemed so far away. "W-we should stop. Addie will be back any second. Besides, I wanted to give you something."

He bit her bottom lip. "Promises, promises."

"I made you something." Sort of. "Wait here."

He stepped back, allowing her to move, but didn't let go of her hand until the last minute. "Did you find your shoe yet?" she called to Addie. When her daughter answered in the affirmative, Layla added, "Need any help tying them?"

Addie insisted she wanted to do it by herself, and Layla ducked into her room to grab the gift bag off her bed. She hadn't thought about wrapping it until after it was finished this afternoon, so she'd asked Gena if she had anything handy…which was why Jace's present was in a large yellow bag with three-dimensional embellishments of blue lace butterflies.

He raised an eyebrow when she handed it to him. "Nice. Very manly."

"I figured real men aren't afraid of their sensitive side," she teased.

Grinning, he reached down into the tissue paper and pulled out the bronze collage frame. Layla had picked out something attractive but simple enough to fit with his rustic decor. His breath hitched, his blue eyes bright with emotion. The man definitely had a sensitive side. "Layla. God, this is so… I don't know what to say." He ran his hand over the edge of the frame reverently.

From where she stood, she couldn't see the photos he was looking at, but of course she knew them by heart.

There were five. In the center was a picture of Addie on her first birthday. Surrounding it were assorted photos of the three of them. An old picture of Jace and Layla, both laughing, as he pushed her in the tire swing when she'd been in sixth grade. Addie's school picture from this year, her adorable grin showing that she'd lost her first baby tooth. There was a selfie Layla had taken the other day on Jarrett's ranch just because the lighting had been so pretty. But her favorite was a picture she'd surreptitiously snapped of Addie and Jace snuggled together on the couch watching a movie. Neither of them was looking at the television screen; instead, Jace had made a comment that caused Addie to giggle and Layla had captured the moment when father and daughter grinned at each other, their smiles so alike it had almost brought tears to her eyes.

"I'm ready!" Addie announced, walking into the kitchen with her sneakers tied. And on the wrong feet. She paused, studying their expressions. "Mama, is Jace sad?"

He swallowed hard, shaking his head. "Just the opposite," he assured her. "Your mom just gave me the best present I ever got in my life. Well, second best. The first best was you."

Addie's forehead crinkled in confusion. "I'm not a present."

"How do you feel when you get a present?" Jace asked her.

"Happy. And excited."

"Well, that's how I feel about you. And, look, here's a picture of you with a bow in your hair." He pointed to her kindergarten portrait. "Bows go on presents, right? Do you think you'd fit in this bag?" He carried the yellow bag over to her and slid it on one arm, making her laugh.

But then she frowned again. "Mama, I thought you said no presents tonight."

"None for us," Layla corrected. "It was Jace's turn."

At that, Jace gave her such a mischievous look that she almost clapped her hand to her forehead. Clearly, the man had another surprise up his sleeve—or his parents did. She wouldn't be surprised if the Trents wanted to shower their new granddaughter with gifts. Layla wasn't sure how to discourage them without seeming ungracious. Maybe it wouldn't be so bad to let Addie accept a couple of gifts that she could take home with her as reminders of her new family.

"We ready to go?" Jace asked.

"Just a sec," Layla told him. "Great job tying your laces, baby, but how about we get these shoes on the right feet?"

While Addie switched the shoes, Jace passed Layla his phone. "I just got this text. How would you like me to answer it?"

Layla glanced down and saw that it was from his sister-in-law Kate. She had twins who were just a little bit older than Addie and wanted to know whether she should bring them, to give Addie kids to talk to, or leave them home with their teenage brother, so as not to overwhelm Addie with too many new people in one night. Layla was touched by the thoughtfulness. The Trents really were special people. In time, she wanted her daughter to meet all of them, but it was best to go slowly. Considering that mention of Skyler earlier today had just made Addie homesick for her friends and classmates, maybe it was better not to bring the twins tonight. She texted Kate back a quick reply, then helped Addie into her coat.

The three of them set off for their family outing, and she was in such a good mood she felt like laughing for no reason at all other than sheer happiness.

"Something funny?" Jace asked.

"Not exactly. I was feeling a little blue earlier, but you seem to have cured that."

"Dr. Jace Trent. My parents will be so proud." He winked at her. "Prepare to have fun. I promise you a night to remember."

Layla leaned back in her chair, too stuffed to ever move again. So much for going home. Someone would just have to bring her camera to her; she'd open up a new photo studio in Gayle Trent's dining room. Jace hadn't been exaggerating when he'd promised his mom was a fantastic cook.

Gayle had even coaxed a skeptical Addie to try some of the zucchini casserole, promising her a slice of the world's best pineapple upside-down cake if she ate a little bit of it. While Addie had pronounced the dessert yummy, she looked as if she was going to fall asleep before she even finished her piece. Tonight had been a lot of excitement for her to process. When they'd arrived, Harvey Trent invited Addie to sit next to him and watch the opening of *The Wizard of Oz* while the adults set the table and finished dinner preparations. Then Aunt Kate had sung an entertaining—if melodramatic—rendition of "Somewhere Over the Rainbow" with Addie. During dinner, Addie's new uncles alternated tornado facts with silly stories about Jace as a kid—even as Jace spluttered that at least half of them were fictitious.

Jace and his family had given them a near-perfect evening, and tomorrow night she planned to thoroughly express her gratitude at their grown-up slumber party. There definitely wouldn't be much slumber taking place.

He squeezed her hand under the table, and she grinned at him, impressed that she'd already had such good taste in men at seventeen. Not every woman could say that, but Jace was proving himself worthy of her love. Was it too soon to tell him that she loved him? She wasn't even sure how many dates they'd technically had, but she knew she didn't want to leave Cupid's Bow without saying it.

Jace cleared his throat. "Um, could I have everyone's attention? I'd like to make a toast."

Cole snickered. "Traditionally, that's done at the *beginning* of the meal, little brother. Before everyone's glasses are empty."

"Well, Layla and I aren't afraid to buck convention, are we, beautiful?"

She sheepishly sank down in her chair. It had taken her an hour tonight to feel comfortable again with his parents, facing them after what she'd done. She would have preferred Jace not remind everyone of their unorthodox family situation.

He stood, raising his less-than-half-full glass. "Cole, Will, I made toasts at both your weddings—"

"Don't remind us," Will grumbled. "They weren't so much 'toasts' as public airings of brotherly secrets better left unshared."

Megan laughed. "Don't mind him, Jace. *I* thought your wedding toast was funny."

Jace winked at his sister-in-law. "Anyway, for the last few months, I've wondered if it would ever be my turn—if I would get a chance at the same kind of happiness you two lucky bastards have found."

"Language!" Gayle reprimanded.

"Sorry, Ma. I had more I wanted to say, but since my family seems intent on interrupting me at every turn, I'd better make this quick. Addie Rose, you told me earlier this week that you didn't want to stay at my house without your mom, and I think you're onto something. I think we should all be together."

"Wait, what?" Layla had been amused by his family's banter, but when he brought Addie into the toast, faint alarm bells sounded in the back of her head. If he wanted to discuss the possibility of Layla eventually moving to Cupid's Bow, they should have had that conversation privately, not with an audience.

He pulled a black velvet box from his pocket, stamped with the logo of the local jewelry store, and there were gasps around the table as he popped it open, offering a sparkling diamond ring toward Layla.

Addie clapped her hands. "Mommy, you get a present, too!"

Oh, no. This wasn't a gift she could accept—not here, not now. What did he think he was doing?

"Layla Anne Dempsey, will you marry me?"

Her throat was closing. She couldn't breathe. Dark pinpoints danced in her vision as she felt all eyes on her.

"Mama?"

Layla didn't know whether the questioning note in her daughter's tone was because Addie wanted to know her answer or if her daughter was confused about what was happening.

Luckily Megan, who'd been a single mother of three for years before she met Will, was good with kids and quickly interceded. "Hey, Addie, I got here too late to watch the good part of *The Wizard of Oz* with you. Can we go restart it, give your mom a chance to thank Jace for his present?"

Addie grimaced. "You mean kiss him again?"

Hell. Addie had seen that? Which time? More than once? Layla thought they'd been discreet. Of course, she'd also thought this might be her and Jace's second date and now he *was proposing*, so what did she know?

"Here." Someone—Kate, she thought—pressed a cold glass of water into Layla's hand. "Drink a little bit of this."

"And maybe put your head between your knees," Cole advised.

"She's fine," Jace insisted. "I just caught her by surprise. Right, Layla?"

Understatement of the century. She was too dizzy to nod, though. Dimly aware of the others filing out of the room, Layla sipped her water, mentally willing her pulse to slow. From the living room, she heard the MGM lion roar, followed by the orchestral score of opening credits she'd long ago memorized. They were playing the movie louder than necessary, probably to give Jace and Layla some degree of privacy, but the dining room felt claustrophobic. Ten minutes ago, she'd been so contentedly full that she couldn't imagine ever moving from her chair; now she couldn't wait to get the hell out of here.

"I need some air," she said.

The spots in front of her eyes were slowly fading, but she barely saw her surroundings as Jace led her out the back door. The night air was blessedly cool. She leaned on the deck railing, trying to catch her breath.

"Well. That did not go the way I envisioned," he said wryly. "It was a little embarrassing, actually."

"For you?" She gaped at him, marveling at how obtuse he was. *Lord, I hope Addie got my brains.*

"Of course for me." His chuckle was self-deprecating. "When a guy lays it all on the line like that, he hopes a girl will say yes, especially when there's an audience. But you don't need to be embarrassed because you got momentarily overwhelmed. It was a dramatic moment. I'm sure everyone understands."

Her jaw dropped. There were so many flaws with what he'd said that she didn't even know where to begin. He shouldn't have asked in front of an audience. He shouldn't have asked, period. "Jace, I don't *like* dramatic moments. How many times have I complained to you about my family drama or told you that I try to keep excess drama away from Addie?"

His brow furrowed, as if he were trying to translate her words from another language. "Well, yeah, but that's a different kind of drama. This was romantic."

"Not really." She no longer felt faint, but she didn't have the mental energy to formulate a diplomatic response. "You didn't start with all the things you liked about me or why we're good together. You started by admitting that you were jealous of what your brothers have. You've recently identified a hole in your life, and Addie and I conveniently fill it. But we won't be as convenient once we leave town, so you tried to keep us here."

"And *I'm* dramatic?" His face darkened. "I didn't try to lock you in a tower, Layla, I asked you to spend your life with me."

"Which is ridiculous! You've never even told me you love me. I've never said it to you."

"But you do, don't you? That picture collage you gave me earlier… I looked at it and I saw family, *my* family."

Part of her liked that explanation and wanted to cling to it, but he hadn't magically conjured an engagement ring on the ride over here. He'd already decided to do it, and the more she thought about it, the more she doubted their compatibility. He was so impulsive. When they'd been kids, there'd been nothing like Jace's spontaneity to liven up a boring summer day. But they were adults now with responsibilities, with a child. His sister-in-law, a woman Layla barely knew, had thought ahead to text and ask about whether to bring her twins, whether it would be best for Addie. But Jace had proposed right in front of their daughter with seemingly no concern for how she would react.

Tears pricked her eyes. She didn't want the first time she said she loved him to be because he'd badgered her into the admission. Right now, she was so disappointed in him it was hard to tell how she felt. "I need time to think it over. And space. And what about Addie's needs? At your house, she got freaked out by a comforter and a ceiling fan. It didn't occur to you that suggesting a massive life change and uprooting her from the only home she's ever known might freak her out? What if she hates the idea of us getting married? Or, even if she's all for it, how dare you give her false hope when you didn't know what I'd say?"

"I hoped you would say yes—obviously—but I should have known better. Because here you are, running away," he growled. "Again."

She sucked in a breath, crossing her arms in front of

her as if to shield herself against his words. "That was a low blow. Don't act like I'm scared of commitment. I'm not the one who dropped out of college—which I never actually went to, since I was busy raising a baby—then quit a dozen jobs and broke up with twice as many girls. What you call running away is just me having the good sense to avoid things that hurt me, like parents teaching toddlers the concept of 'too hot.' Addie and I are leaving Cupid's Bow, not because I'm some kind of coward, but because it was *always* the plan. It's logical. Not sticking around to get burned more by you is just a bonus."

When the back door opened behind him an hour later, Jace regretted staying on the back deck instead of just getting in his truck and leaving—but that would have been the Layla response to a situation, to run off without having to face his family. He'd been here since Addie came to hug him goodbye, informing him that Aunt Kate was giving them a ride home. He hadn't known what to say to his little girl regarding the botched proposal, and she hadn't mentioned it, so he'd dropped the subject for the time being. After she'd gone, he'd sat down to wait for the hurt and humiliation to fade, staring out across his parents' property and seriously considering chucking the ring in his pocket into the tree line.

Apparently, his family had decided they'd left him alone long enough.

"I'm not good company," he said to whomever was behind him.

"True," Cole said. "But that's never stopped us from hanging out with you before." He sat down on Jace's right.

Will sat on the left, handing Jace a chilled bottle of beer, already opened.

Jace took a swig, working up the nerve to ask, "Was she okay? When she left?" Without even looking at them, he could feel his brothers exchange glances, knew they were silently deciding how to answer and who should answer. Cole and Will had always been close; they could damn near communicate through telepathy.

"She was trying very hard not to cry," Will said.

"But Kate hasn't come back yet," Cole added. "Between Kate and Gena, they'll make sure she's all right. Kate might even put in a good word for you."

Would there be any point? "The family screwup strikes again."

Will bopped him on the head. "Quit feeling sorry for yourself."

Jace glared. "Don't the two of you ever worry about causing me permanent brain injury?"

"That would explain your actions tonight," Cole said. "What the hell were you thinking, bro?"

"Not you, too! Layla already made me feel like a dumbass for asking in front of an audience." He wasn't sure why that was a mistake. People accepted marriage proposals in public all the time. He'd personally witnessed at least three in the town gazebo during various festivals.

"I wasn't talking about the audience so much as the timing," Cole said. "You had to know she would be nervous about seeing Mom and Dad for the first time after them learning that she gave birth to their granddaughter. You didn't think maybe one major milestone event might be enough for the night?"

It had seemed perfect in his head, all the people he

loved most together in one room. *You've never even told me you love me.* Hadn't he? He felt like he had. He felt like it was so glaringly obvious every time he looked at her, every time he touched her, that half the town probably knew by now. But, based on what she'd said tonight, he wasn't sure she felt the same way.

Despair clawed at him, a desperation to chase after her and talk some sense into her, convince her how good they would be together. "I can fix this," he said aloud. "I just caught her off guard. I was impulsive, and she overreacted, but—"

"Whoa. I'm just gonna stop you there," Will said. "You will never 'fix' things with a woman by telling her she overreacted."

"Never," Cole seconded.

Will was shaking his head. "Not ever."

"I get the point, guys. I'm not an idiot."

"No," Cole agreed, "but you aren't the world's best listener, and you don't always think before you act."

"Hey, whose side are you on?" Jace demanded. That decided it—Will was definitely his favorite brother. Until the next time Will whacked him on the head, anyway. "You two don't understand—"

Cole threw his head back and laughed. On the other side of Jace, Will spluttered beer.

"Nothing about this is funny," Jace said darkly.

"Oh, come on. You don't think we've both been exactly where you are now?" Cole challenged. "Do you not remember when Kate was too scared to be with me because she thought my job was dangerous? Or that not-so-festive Christmas when Will moped an entire day because he was afraid he'd lost Megan?"

"Damn," Will said softly, "maybe we really *have*

caused him brain damage. Jace, how long have you been having these gaps in your memory?"

"He probably doesn't remember," Cole deadpanned.

Jace got to his feet. "You two suck. I'm in *pain* here. Cole, the first time you became a father, you had nine months to get used to the idea. I've had less than nine weeks. I'm not perfect, okay? But I love that little girl, and I love her exasperating mother, and I'm *losing* them."

"Maybe that's for the best," Cole said. "Wait— Hear me out! I just mean that maybe a little time and space will be beneficial to you both. When I couldn't convince Kate to accept my job, do you remember what I did? I let her go. And it was awful, worse than the time I got stabbed on a 10-16 call. But the time apart was what we needed to come back together stronger than ever."

"Layla and I already had our time apart." They'd been together seven years ago. *This* had been their second chance, and she didn't want it. Maybe she never would. His gut reaction had been to keep trying, to persuade her to change her mind, but that had only pushed her further away.

She'd implied he wasn't *logical*. Maybe the most logical thing he could do was learn from his mistakes and know when to walk away from a no-win situation.

Chapter 15

"We hate to see you go so soon," Suzanne said, hugging Layla tightly.

"Soon?" Layla echoed. She could barely remember a time before this trip. It had turned her life upside down and normalcy was a vague memory. "The only reason Addie and I haven't already overstayed our welcome is because Gena is some kind of guardian angel. Anyone else would have kicked us to the curb by now. Besides, as I promised Mom, we'll be back. Definitely for the holidays, if not sooner." At the moment, the thought of seeing Jace again made her queasy, but he and Addie had begun to forge a bond; Layla had no intention of keeping them apart.

"When you do come back, you're welcome to stay with us," Suzanne said. She walked over to where Addie sat by the playpen, explaining tornados to the babies, to say goodbye, leaving Layla with alone with Chris.

She squeezed her brother's uninjured hand. "I have a couple of things to tell you. Your friends and I banded together on a little fund-raising project. I had been planning to show it to you in person, but there's been a slight production delay and I need to go. Just know, when you see it, that it was done with love and humor, and we all wanted to find a way to help."

Chris raised an eyebrow. "Production delay? I don't know whether I'm grateful or scared."

"I think both are appropriate. And there's something else... I wouldn't even mention it, but with this being Cupid's Bow, you might hear from someone else. In a moment of insanity, your friend Jace asked me to marry him."

"Seriously? That's fantas—"

"No, no, no. It was a mistake. It's behind us now."

Chris frowned. "Wait. Is that why you're leaving?"

"I don't know why people keep asking me about my reasons for leaving. I don't actually live here! I was always planning to leave. Going back to my house and my job and Addie's school isn't running away."

"Okay, okay. Sorry, I didn't mean anything by it. I just...like having you around."

"Well, I'll make you a deal. You promise not to let any more seventeen-hundred-pound bulls step on you, and I promise to visit more."

He chuckled. "Solid plan. So, when you do visit again, do you and Jace have more milk shake dates planned?"

"No. I want him to be part of Addie's life, but... At the end of the day, he and I are two very different people."

She'd called last night to tell him she and Addie were

headed out this morning. She'd assured him he was welcome to call his daughter but that it might be best if they developed a weekly schedule, rather than his randomly checking in during the middle of dinner or disrupting her bedtime routine. The conversation had been awkward and stilted, and he'd been almost unrecognizably cold to her. He was clearly angry she was leaving, which infuriated her. She could have left without any word at all, but she'd reached out, tried to be an adult about the situation. By the end of the conversation, she was snapping at him, a sarcastic version of herself she didn't particularly like and not a great role model for her daughter. She didn't want a future with an impulsive man-child who lashed out when he didn't get his way.

Maybe one day, after enough time had passed, she and Jace could rebuild their friendship. In the meantime, it would have to be enough that Addie knew she had a father who loved her. And whatever hope Layla had held that he might love her, too? She would work hard to forget it.

Moving on was the reasonable, adult thing to do, and Addie should have at least one sensible parent.

There'd been a time when the tantalizing smell of barbecue would have made Jace's stomach growl loud enough for the cooks in the kitchen to hear. But as he stood in the carryout line of the Smoky Pig, all he wanted was to get the order and get to the solitude of his truck. He might scream if one more smiling person asked, "Hey, how's it going?"

So much for thinking that getting out of the store for a few minutes would improve his mood. Tonight was a special after-hours inventory, and Grayson's girlfriend had joined them to help. Jace had volunteered to pick up dinner for the three of them as an excuse to get away from the happy couple. He liked Hadley just fine, but right now, watching their shared glances and casual touches made him want to put a fist through the wall.

I wanted that. He'd shot for the same kind of happiness—and he'd been shot down.

People in Cupid's Bow thought of Jace as a perpetual bachelor, but when he'd found the person he could see himself sharing his life with, she'd bolted. Layla could have asked for more time to think it over; she could have said no, it's too soon, ask again in three months. Or six. Instead, she'd yelled at him, told him he wasn't romantic and accused him of not caring about what was best for Addie.

Then she'd called him earlier this week to tell him she was leaving town even sooner than originally discussed. Their final conversation had held all the warmth and intimacy of making an appointment at the dentist's office. Had he been mistaken all along about his feelings for her? Maybe his judgment had been clouded by the memory of the fearless, free-spirited girl he'd once known. People changed. He admired Layla, but she was skittish and rigid now.

He sent a silent, wistful apology to seventeen-year-old Layla Dempsey. It seemed he finally loved her back, but he was nearly a decade too late.

"I've got her," Martin offered as Layla reached for her sleeping daughter. "It's been weeks since I tucked her in. Let me carry her to bed while I can still lift her. These old bones aren't getting any younger, and she's growing."

"Like a weed," Layla agreed ruefully. Addie had left

the house today in another pair of pants that looked like they'd suddenly shrunk two inches. Hopefully, people at school had mistaken them for capris. "Thanks, Dad."

As Martin took his snoring granddaughter down the hall, Layla turned off the television. This was the third night in a row Addie had fallen asleep while watching *Twister*. She found the action-packed "flying cow movie" paradoxically soothing. Layla, on the other hand, could barely get through it without crying. And she was afraid her dad had noticed.

As owner of the modest brick duplex, Martin was technically Layla's landlord and neighbor. He had his own adjacent residence, but he'd been spending almost all his time at Layla's since her return. He said it was because he'd missed Addie so much and wanted to hear about her adventures at school, but Layla hadn't missed her father's concerned glances. He thought she was suffering from a broken heart.

He's right. Not that it mattered. Layla had gotten over Jace Trent before, and she could damn well do it again.

Moments later, her dad padded back into the room. "How about I make us some hot cocoa?"

She grinned. "Like when I was a little girl."

"I'm glad you remember. Truth is, I was such a crappy dad, I wasn't sure how many good memories you had of me."

"Daddy, we do not need to go through this again. I don't know how Addie and I would have survived without your help the first few years. Whatever came before that, I forgave you a long time ago."

"Which is more than I deserve," her father said heavily, "but forgiving isn't the same as forgetting. All the mistakes I made as a dad are still there somewhere, deep down, *and* the mistakes I made as a husband. I worry sometimes... You don't date much."

"I'm a single mother and a small business owner."

"I know, honey. But it can't be easy to commit when your own parents' marriage was such a train wreck. I wasn't sorry things with that Kyle fellow never got serious, but if there comes a day when a man wants to marry you, I—"

The house was so quiet that her sob echoed all around them. She clapped a hand over her mouth as if she could somehow take it back.

"Layla? What is it?"

"Nothing. I..." Another sob. And another.

Dammit, she'd tried so hard to stifle these unproductive feelings. There were better ways to spend her time than crying over a guy who'd hurt her and callously refused to see her point of view. But that didn't stop the hot tears dripping off her cheeks and chin.

Her father handed her a tissue box and left the room. Moments later, he returned with a mug of hot chocolate, no doubt half full of marshmallows. His cocoa-to-mallow ratio had always been a little skewed.

She managed a watery smile. "Thanks. I'm better now."

"Was it something I said? Or was it Jace Trent?"

"Both?" She blew across the surface of steamy marshmallow froth. "He, uh, kind of proposed before I came back to Austin. But the timing was terrible and we've never even discussed the future—"

"Some might assume raising a child together implies a future."

"Well, it shouldn't. If I get married, I want it to be because someone loves me." That stupid proposal. Jace hadn't once claimed to love her. She wasn't sure it was even possible to love someone you were so disdainful of—every time she needed to take a beat and distance herself from a situation, he basically called her a coward. Love meant respecting your partner's needs and personality, even if it was different from yours.

Oh, hell.

She squeezed her eyes shut. Did loving Jace mean that she should have shown more respect for *his* personality? Was it fair for her to criticize his tendency for showmanship and surprises when she'd so often benefited from them?

She recalled Addie's glowing expression when he'd first shown up with his handmade tornado machine. And what about the afternoon he'd abruptly announced to her family that he was Addie's father? It hadn't been his place to share that news. Yet, he'd done it out of concern for her, and it had been a welcome resolution to a situation so unpleasant she'd felt as if she were suffocating.

"Why do you think he proposed?" her father asked gently. "Just for Addie's sake?"

"No," she admitted. "But whatever his motivations, it was awful. Jace likes bold gestures. Sometimes, they're nice, but other times they backfire. And if I always have to point those backfires out to him, I'm the bad guy." He would always be the one telling Addie yes, she could have one more story or an additional dessert or watch a movie Layla vetoed, which relegated her to disciplinarian. Both her daughter and her lover would come to resent her.

"You said yourself some of the gestures are nice," her father pointed out. "Maybe the two of you can reach compromises over time."

"That's what I thought! But he didn't give me time." No, he'd wanted to make a splashy statement in front of his family to prove he could be like his big brothers. "The thing is, Dad, Jace lives his life based on impulse. He blurts things out, he shows up out of the blue, he springs surprises on people. Whoever he does marry, she's in for a lifetime of spontaneous celebrations and spur-of-the-moment romantic escapes. But what about when his impulse is to walk away? What about those day-to-day moments that aren't fun? Is he going to stick by a woman he doesn't understand, or get bored and wander off?"

Her dad looked sheepish.

"I'm not only worried because you left mom. It's also because I know Jace. He doesn't have a track record of sticking with things. What if he can't change?"

"Life doesn't come with guarantees, honey. But ask yourself this—if he changed too much, would he still be the man you love? Nobody is perfect. If you can learn to accept occasional flaws, though, you might find more happiness than you thought possible."

"GC Tack and Supply, Jace speaking."

"Just the man I was lookin' for," a female voice drawled. "This is Mona, callin' to let you know your shipment of calendars is printed and ready to pick up."

Jace's jaw clenched. Calendars. Layla. Pain flooded him. Every day, he woke up somewhat numb, convinced he was making progress in getting over her. And every single day, there was something that reminded him he was a liar. "Great. I'll run over during lunch today and pick them up." Might as well—with his recent lack of appetite, it wasn't as if he actually needed a lunch break.

A few minutes after twelve, he parked in the alley behind Mona's store to load up his cargo. He and Grayson had committed to trying to sell half a dozen boxes. Frankly, Jace would rather never think about the calendars again—or about the sensual afternoon he and Layla had spent together when he'd hijacked his business partner's scheduled photo shoot—but these were to help Chris. Jace still cared about his friend and knew the sales could make a big difference for Chris and Suzanne.

"Thanks, Mona."

Her grin was openly appreciative. "Thank *you*. And all the other guys, too. These calendars are fantastic. I know Jarrett and Hugh are married, and Grayson is taken, but after women get a load of these pictures? You and Quincy will have ladies linin' up at your doors to date you."

Yippee.

Bad attitude, Trent. You should want *to date again.* Right. He just had to remember the goal—find someone who appreciated him. How hard could that be?

When he got back to the store, Hadley had dropped by with lunch for Grayson. The two of them were talking in low voices in the management office. He could hear Grayson's low, mischievous tone and Hadley's occasional giggles through the wall. He hated to interrupt, but he needed a place to put the boxes. Leaving things lying around for customers to randomly trip over was, generally speaking, a bad idea.

Hadley caught sight of him and did an excited double take at the boxes. "Are those the calendars? Oooh!" She reached to grab a pair of scissors from Grayson's desk. "I cannot wait to see these."

Grayson shot a questioning glance at Jace. "Did they

turn out okay? Do I look stupid? Am I going to regret this?"

"Honestly? I haven't seen them yet," Jace said. "But Layla is pretty good at her job, so…" Even saying her name stung. He *hated* this. When was it going to get better?

Hadley had ripped into a box and pulled out the top copy. "Ohmigosh. Y'all look like real models. I mean, these pictures are…" She flipped through the calendar, stopping a couple of pages in. "Would it be wrong to blow this up into a giant poster for my house?"

Grayson laughed. "What do you need the poster for when you can have the real-life version any time you want?"

Jace slipped out of the office, taking one of the calendars with him. *Go ahead and look.* It wasn't as if Layla was *in* the pictures. He should just get this over with so he didn't react when customers asked questions, fanned through the images or even good-naturedly ribbed him about his participation. The cover was a picture of a few shirts draped over a fence on a sunny day; Jace's hat topped the fence post. He remembered that day at the Twisted R. It had been right after Layla said they shouldn't kiss again, yet she hadn't been able to keep from blushing every time she'd looked in his direction.

The first photo was a group shot. She'd done a good job. Objectively speaking, they looked like an attractive bunch of guys without it being too cheesy or risqué. They looked like exactly what they were—Texas cowboys with their shirts off, not male strippers. Then there were individual shots, black-and-white portraits interspersed with color. His black-and-white photo was a profile shot, and it was artistic, the kind of thing his parents could show their friends with pride. When he reached the other picture of himself, he stopped cold, struck by the image. It was like looking at a stranger who wore his face.

The man in the photo was staring straight into the camera, and his grin was startling. It was so personal. Jace hadn't been smiling for the camera, he'd been smiling at her. And he knew in his gut, he hadn't smiled like that since the night she'd turned down his proposal. He'd once jokingly thought about going to the top of the Cupid's Bow water tower and announcing to the entire town how he felt about Layla Dempsey. When people started buying copies of this calendar, he wouldn't have to— they'd all know just from his expression.

You love her.

So what was he going to do about it?

Even with the calendar project that had put her behind a camera, Layla had missed working in her studio while she was away. She loved it here. It wasn't just where she performed her job; it was physical proof of her hard-won professional success. Except, on this particular Friday, the studio was also the site of engagement photos for a happy couple. There had been a split second during their session when Layla had ever-so-briefly fantasized about bashing the next person who said "love you more" with a tripod.

Thank goodness they'd been her last appointment of the day. She was too cranky to do her job well. *Not because you miss Jace! You're cranky because you didn't get enough sleep.* Chris has called her last night, calendar in hand. He'd been both touched by everyone's efforts on his behalf and amused by his friends' attempts at modeling. "Think any of them will remember me when they all go off and become famous?" he'd teased.

After she'd hung up with her grateful brother, she'd pulled up the calendar proofs on her laptop. Even knowing it was a bad idea, she hadn't been able to help herself. She'd stared long and hard at the pictures of Jace as if she could use his image to practice what she wanted to say next time she saw him in person.

I'm sorry. I love you. You're a self-centered dummy who should have more empathy for how I felt.

I miss you so much.

The studio phone rang, and Layla dropped into her desk chair to answer, grateful for the distraction even though she should have let the machine get it. She was headed out any minute for afternoon carpool at the elementary school. Checking the lone-star clock that hung over the reception area, she rattled off her usual greeting automatically, ending with, "How may I help you?"

"Knock-knock."

She almost dropped the phone. *"Jace?"*

"I told you once that I'd learn some knock-knock jokes for you, remember?"

"I… What are you talking about?" Her mind couldn't process that he had called her. On her business line, no less. He had her cell number.

"I want to start over."

"That's probably a good idea." She rubbed her temple. "I'm sorry— Maybe it's just because I didn't get much sleep, but I'm having a little trouble following this conversation."

"No, I mean, I want *us* to start over. I miss you, Layla. So much it hurts."

Tears stung her eyes. *Me, too.* She tried to say the

words, but it was hard to get them past the lump of emotion in her throat.

"Opening with the knock-knock joke was a lame idea," he said, "but it would have worked better if you'd responded, *Who's there?* Still, I told you once that I'd learn some for you, and that's my point. I *can* learn, beautiful. The old Jace would have stormed up to your house and announced his feelings for the entire neighborhood to hear, but I wanted to show restraint. I didn't ambush you, didn't call your personal number. If you want to take it slow, or if you don't want to see me..." He stumbled a bit over that, but regained his composure. "I'm sorry if I made you feel like I can't respect your wishes. I'll work on it, Layla. I—"

"I love you," she blurted. "Please don't change too much, because I love you. I've been trying not to, trying to move past it, but—"

"Sucks, doesn't it?" His laugh was rusty. "I tried, too. It's freaking impossible."

In what was beginning to feel like a daily occurrence, her face was once again damp with tears. But for the first time since she'd left Cupid's Bow, they were happy tears. She sniffed. "I'm so glad you called. I was already trying to figure out what to say to you, and—"

"Really?"

"I practiced with your picture. How's that for lame?"

"I love you, too."

She rocked back in the chair, overcome with joy. Her dad had been right—if you wanted the rewards, you had to be willing to take the risks. Jace was more than worth it. They might not always agree on everything, but she didn't have one single doubt in her mind that she loved him. The rest of it, they could work on together. "I miss you. What's your weekend like? It's kind of a long drive, but maybe—"

Click.

"Jace? You still there?" When there was no answer, she glanced at the digital readout on her receiver. Call Ended.

There was a chime as the door of her studio opened, and she was about to announce that they were closed when Jace strode inside.

"Knock-knock," he said hoarsely. He was unshaven and he'd lost about ten pounds and no man on the planet had ever looked better.

She flew out of her chair so fast it wobbled, the wheeled base the only thing that kept it from tipping over. "You're here," she breathed, launching herself into a hug.

"Couldn't stay away." He caught her midtackle. "Unless you had wanted me to, in which case I would have worked hard to give you what you needed. Thank God that's not what you needed."

She nuzzled his neck. "You smell so good."

"Like road trip and desperation?"

"Like *you.*"

He kissed her, and the grainy, out-of-focus world she'd been existing in was suddenly high resolution again and full of promise. Her lips parted beneath his, and she kissed him back eagerly, wishing she had time to drag him home with her for a few hours of getting reacquainted. But carpool loomed.

Regretfully, she pulled away. "Addie—"

"We don't have to tell her I'm in town yet," he said earnestly. "Not if you think—"

"I was going to say, Addie is about to get out of

school. Otherwise, we'd still be kissing. Actually, I'd have you naked by now."

He grinned. "Oh, yeah?"

"Do you, uh, have plans for where you're going to spend the night?" she asked, suddenly shy. Having him here was different than being with him in Cupid's Bow, home of their shared past. Jace driving all this way to tell her how he felt, continually checking to make sure he wasn't bulldozing her... The future had never looked brighter.

"I'm flexible," he told her. "I'll go home to Cupid's Bow if I need to, or book a hotel room or sleep in my truck. I suppose leasing an apartment in Austin by the end of the day is unrealistic?"

"Would you really consider living here?"

"What matters most to me isn't where I sleep tonight or any other night. All I care about is finally falling asleep without the hollow dread that's been consuming me, waking up mornings with the knowledge that we love each other and that I'm earning that love. Layla, I'm sorry. I reacted badly when you turned down my proposal. I was so defensive and hurt that I didn't truly hear what you were saying. Cole's right—sometimes I'm a terrible listener."

"I could have handled it better," she admitted. "You weren't completely wrong about me being scared. Watching my parents' marriage implode left me more guarded than I realized. But someone recently pointed out that life doesn't come with guarantees. Do I want to obsess over what-ifs and be alone, or do I want to be with the only man I've ever loved?"

His grip on her tightened, his blue eyes brilliant. "Really?"

She gave him a lopsided smile. "I don't have a ring. Or an audience. But… Jace Trent, will you marry me? It should probably be a long engagement, but—"

He gave his answer in the form of a kiss, his hands settling on her hips as his mouth claimed hers in a thorough, seductive exploration that sent tingles up her spine.

"You just tell me where and when," he murmured. "I'll wait as long as I have to."

"There will still be times I get scared," she warned him.

"That's okay. I can't promise I won't occasionally get overzealous. But I *can* promise to love you and Addie with all my heart."

"We're lucky to have you." If their life together was never perfect, it was still going to be pretty damn good.

He pressed his forehead to hers. "Family pizza night?"

Family. That's what they were now, what they'd been destined to be. It was a future they would build together. "Let's go pick up our daughter, see what she thinks about Mommy and Daddy living together someday and if she wants to watch the flying cow movie."

Jace laughed, the picture of contentment, and her heart swelled. "I'm just honored to be in the same sentence as the cow."

* * * * *

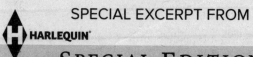
When Matt looked up, she offered him a shy smile. "Like I said, I'm sorry. I should have told you that you were a father."

"You've got that right."

"I've made mistakes, but Emily isn't one of them. She's a great kid. So for now, let's focus on her."

"All right." Matt uncrossed his arms and raked a hand through his hair. "But just for the record, I would've done anything in my power to take care of you and Emily."

"I know." And that was why she'd walked away from him. Matt would have stood up to her father, challenged his threat, only to be knocked to his knees—and worse.

No, leaving town and cutting all ties with Matt was the only thing she could've done to protect him.

As she stood in the room where their daughter was conceived, as she studied the only man she'd ever loved, the memories crept up on her…the old feelings, too.

When she was sixteen, there'd been something about the fun-loving nineteen-year-old cowboy that had drawn her attention. And whatever it was continued to tug at her now. But she shook it off. Too many years had passed; too many tears had been shed.

Besides, an unwed single mother who was expecting another man's baby wouldn't stand a chance with a champion bull rider who had his choice of pretty cowgirls. And she'd best not forget that.

"Aw, hell," Matt said, as he ran a hand through his hair again and blew out a weary sigh. "Maybe you did Emily a favor by leaving when you did. Who knows what kind of father I would have made back then. Or even now."

Don't miss
The Cowboy's Secret Family *by Judy Duarte,*
available June 2019 wherever
Harlequin® Special Edition books and ebooks are sold.

www.Harlequin.com

Need an adrenaline rush from nail-biting tales
(and irresistible males)?

Check out **Harlequin Intrigue®**,
Harlequin® Romantic Suspense and
Love Inspired® Suspense books!

New books available every month!

CONNECT WITH US AT:

Facebook.com/groups/HarlequinConnection

Facebook.com/HarlequinBooks

Twitter.com/HarlequinBooks

Instagram.com/HarlequinBooks

Pinterest.com/HarlequinBooks

ReaderService.com

**ROMANCE WHEN
YOU NEED IT**

SGENRE2018R

Looking for more satisfying love stories
with community and family at their core?

Check out **Harlequin® Special Edition**
and **Love Inspired®** books!

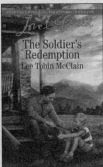

New books available every month!

CONNECT WITH US AT:

Facebook.com/groups/HarlequinConnection

Facebook.com/HarlequinBooks

Twitter.com/HarlequinBooks

Instagram.com/HarlequinBooks

Pinterest.com/HarlequinBooks

ReaderService.com

**ROMANCE WHEN
YOU NEED IT**

HFGENRE2018

Looking for inspiration in tales
of hope, faith and heartfelt romance?

Check out **Love Inspired®** and
Love Inspired® Suspense books!

New books available every month!

CONNECT WITH US AT:

Facebook.com/groups/HarlequinConnection

Facebook.com/HarlequinBooks

Twitter.com/HarlequinBooks

Instagram.com/HarlequinBooks

Pinterest.com/HarlequinBooks

ReaderService.com

Love Harlequin romance?

DISCOVER.

Be the first to find out about promotions, news and exclusive content!

f Facebook.com/HarlequinBooks

Twitter.com/HarlequinBooks

Instagram.com/HarlequinBooks

Pinterest.com/HarlequinBooks

ReaderService.com

EXPLORE.

Sign up for the Harlequin e-newsletter and download a free book from any series at **TryHarlequin.com.**

CONNECT.

Join our Harlequin community to share your thoughts and connect with other romance readers!
Facebook.com/groups/HarlequinConnection

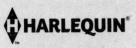

ROMANCE WHEN YOU NEED IT

HSOCIAL2018

Earn points on your purchase of new Harlequin books from participating retailers.

Turn your points into **FREE BOOKS** of your choice!

Join for FREE today at
www.HarlequinMyRewards.com.

Harlequin My Rewards is a free program (no fees) without any commitments or obligations.

MYR18